Field Guide

Field Guide

Essays and Stories

by

Steve Sherwood

ANGELINA
RIVER
PRESS

Fort Worth, Texas

ISBN 978-0-9883844-2-2
Library of Congress Control Number: 2014930087

Angelina River Press, LLC
Fort Worth Texas

Acknowledgments

I am grateful to the editors of the following journals for publishing the essays and stories gathered into this collection:

Amarillo Bay, "Assassinations"
CCTE Studies, "Physical Education"
(A version of "Physical Education" also appeared in *The Clearing House* in January 2013)
The Chiron Review, "Archipelago"
descant, "Swimmer" and "Purple Hearts"
New Texas, "Keepsakes" and "Cage"
Northern Lights, "In the Footsteps of Captain Filth"
Red Rock Review, "Marathon"
RiverSedge, "The Bright Side"
Rendezvous, "Environmentalist as Misanthrope"
Talking River Review, "Field Guide"
Weber Studies, "Wilderness as a Psychic Dumping Ground"

Special thanks to
Dave Kuhne
Jerry Craven
Cynthia Shearer

Other Books from Angelina River Press

Memoirs
Adventures from the Last Century, Carl Craven
Memoirs of a Biologist, Gail Fail

Fiction
The Wild Part, Jerry Craven

www.AngelinaRiverPress.Com

Also by Steve Sherwood
Hardwater
No Asylum

For Ed and Melba Sherwood

CONTENTS

ESSAYS

STORIES

Field Guide

A redwood sprouts seedlings from its trunk when felled by fire or old age. Clones of the tree grow out of its remains, so even though the tree itself dies its genetic code lives on. In this way, redwoods are immortal.

My mother made this observation from the shade of an immortal in Jedediah Smith Redwoods State Park as we watched my sons skip stones across the Smith River. She had offered up natural history lessons, sparked by an ant lion pit or a molting pine snake, since I was a kid. My siblings and I groaned when she knelt to explain the mysteries of the bull thistle or the prickly pear, but in hindsight we could see these lessons had punctuated our childhoods and in my case paid off during a backpack trip in northern Mexico, when I survived for a week on the succulent meat of the prickly pear. Her lesson on the immortality of redwoods caught my attention that day because I thought it might be her last.

Doctors diagnosed the cancer not long after she and my father moved to Oregon. They tasted a year of the sort of retirement couples dream about—walking the rocky beaches, filling jars with sand dollars, watching otters and seals frolic in the cool Pacific. Then there were three years of dire prognoses and radiation treatments. Her cancer afflicted only one lung, but the doctors could not operate because fifty years of smoking had so damaged the "good" lung that it could not sustain her. Radiation, the only option, drove the cancer into hiding and for a time returned to my mother a portion of her energy. As we rested beneath a redwood on the Smith River and watched my sons skip stones across its turquoise waters, she was ten months into remission.

She died a few weeks later. Though monumental to her family, her passing left hardly a ripple in the world. No major newspaper ran her obituary. During her seventy years, she had authored no famous works of literature, won no Nobel Peace Prizes, held no public office above school board. A housewife and mother in the outmoded tradition of the nineteen fifties, she left as evidence of her existence only some photographs and letters, an eclectic collection of books, a husband, five children, eight grandchildren, and whatever memories of her they kept. In most ways, she was a mystery even to those who should have known her better.

Some moments with her remain clear. There's the time she cut the tip of her finger nearly off while chopping meat and, with blood arcing from her hand, muttered reassurances to her children. There's the time she nursed back to health a ruby-throated hummingbird that knocked itself out on our picture window. There's the time she insisted we haul from the Rampart Range, on top of the family station wagon, a weathered piñon stump to grace her garden. There's the time when, at thirteen, I had whined too often and for too long and, with a hard, stinging slap, she told me to grow the hell up. There's the time she forgot to put sugar in the pumpkin pie when, having grown the hell up, I brought home my first serious girlfriend for Thanksgiving. And there's the time she walked around with a fractured wrist for a week to keep one of my sons, who tripped her, from feeling guilty.

None of these glimpses fully describes or defines her, but of the objects she left behind, her worn, faded copy of *A Field Guide to Rocky Mountain Wildflowers* (Craighead, Craighead, and Davis, 1963) may come closest to revealing how she approached her life.

The field guide's heavy cloth cover has, over the decades, separated from the binding. Inside the back cover and on the blank pages that follow the index, my mother jotted lists and charts in which she cross-referenced wildflowers by color, by month of first flowering, and by the page number on which one could find each flower's photograph, line-drawing, or description.

Under April, she lists fairybells (22), dogtooth violet (23), leopard lily (24), yellow fritillary (24), spring beauty (45), chickweed (49), pasqueflower (54), clematis (57), and sugarbowl (57). As I read her lists, I can hear her eager incantation of the names of the first flowers to appear each spring. I turn to the page given for springbeauty and find a bookmark of a desiccated blossom. In red, she underlined the flower's color ("pink or white") and where it grows ("in moist soil from valleys to alpine regions, 10,000-11,000 ft."). A "PP" beside a color photograph on Plate 7 indicates she found the flower somewhere near our former family home in Perry Park, a valley that parallels the Rampart Range of the Colorado Rockies. A "Not CO" next to a species on the same page marks a flower found only in the northern Rockies. A ruddy spot stains the page next to the entry for the alpine primrose, as if she pricked her finger on a thorn.

As I follow the meticulous trail of notes and dried leaves or flowers she left in the book, I also retrace her footsteps through the ponderosa stands and moist meadows that carpet the valley between the granite, forested mountains to the west and the waves of hogback ridges with their red and blond sandstone cliffs to the east of our family home. She often wandered the wildest parts of this valley—a place we both loved, though for different reasons—with book in hand, identifying larkspurs, alpine bluebells, and blue columbines as they sprang from the rocky soil.

My mother loved the finer details of Perry Park. She gathered them with a fervor that reflected a desire to claim the land by learning the names of its trees, flowers, rocks, and creatures. By contrast, I loved the sweep of the place, the adventure and freedom from parents and peers I could find on its rock faces and in its hidden dells. I often climbed to the top of a cliff or hiked the ridgeline of the Rampart Range until I found a place to sit, listen, and watch the shifting light on the valley floor. During my rambles, I sometimes saw the hummingbirds that thrilled my mother, but I also encountered timber rattlers, wild turkeys, great horned owls, black bear, and once in an alcove on a high sandstone ledge a mountain lion, whose blue-green eyes stared into mine until I backed down the cliff. I loved the smell of piñon and ponderosa, the hint of rain on the northwest wind, and the promise of cliff edges and distant peaks. My eyes settled not on flowers but on climbing routes—cracks, traverses, and lines of ascent—and I claimed the land by walking and climbing as much of it as I could. My mother's gaze was far more systematic, fine-tuned by a series of field guides like the one she passed down to me. Not content to wonder about a flower, insect, reptile, bird, or mammal, she would look it up, identify it, and commit its specific traits to memory.

Her desire to learn took her from meadows to mountainsides, often along the High Road, which ran to the mouth Bear Creek Canyon. Sunday mornings, once spent in church, became a time to walk together in the patch of wilderness surrounding our home. Still devout, I wondered about the change until my mother revealed her existential views. On one walk, when I asked what she believed about heaven, hell, and life after death, she hesitated, perhaps unwilling to inflict her beliefs on me. She looked around us and asked, "What could be better than this?" Pressed, she admitted she saw death as a natural end—when you die you simply die—and the only immortality she hoped for was to live on through her children. Heaven and hell, if they existed, were right here on Earth.

As she walked through her version of heaven, she bent often to get a closer look at yellow columbines, rosy quartz crystals, praying mantises, mosses and lichens, lines of marauding ants, and beaver skulls. She turned

3

rocks, shells, yucca pods, pinecones, and the lost feathers of owls or hawks into works of art that hung on our walls. By keeping her eyes on the ground, she also recovered such manmade rarities as Ute spear points and lengths of antique barbed wire, equipped with rowels instead of barbs.

Her self-education turned her into a naturalist. By subtle tricks of persuasion, she tried to do the same for us. She started us young, in Kansas. I have early memories of watching, each morning at breakfast, a pair of cardinals build a nest and start a family in a tree outside our kitchen window in Wichita. Encouraged by our mother, we witnessed the hatching and growth of the chicks until, one morning, a large snake coiled in the branches around the nest, its neck bulging and its eyes black as the cardinals swooped and fluttered to drive it away.

This mealtime lesson on nature's food chain, perhaps harsher than intended, led to a fascination with snakes, which my brother Brian and I sometimes caught in the yard. Our mother forced us to release them unharmed, saying snakes had as much right to live as any creature, but an incident in Colorado Springs, where we moved a few years later, tested her tolerance. We were playing catch in the yard when we heard tires skidding on the gravel road in front of our house. The driver of a pickup kicked up dust as he backed over a large rattlesnake in the road, stopped, shifted gears, and rolled over the snake again. He got out, and we went over for a look. Warning us to keep our distance, he explained that he'd seen the rattler, as thick as his arm, crossing toward our yard and feared for our safety. Half crushed, and unable to rattle its tail, the snake still bobbed its head, ready to strike.

Our mother hurried over from the garden, armed with a hoe. The rattler's body wriggled and its jaws snapped long after she severed its head. Eight years old at the time, I came away from this experience with a deep fear of rattlesnakes, powerful enough to survive being run over by a truck, and with a deeper admiration for my mother, powerful enough to kill such a creature. I wondered about her right to kill versus the snake's right to live, but I also understood she had broken her own rule to protect us. In an international field guide to reptiles, which she provided, Brian and I not only read about western diamondbacks but also about the world's largest and most venomous species—and took comfort in learning there lived in Colorado nothing as large as the Burmese python or as deadly as the black mamba.

At the time, we did not suspect our mother was instilling in us her method of following curiosity to arrive at knowledge. If something mystified us, we usually sought answers from her, our personal field guide. Gradually, we turned to books. Our sisters followed their own interests— music, gymnastics, tennis, archaeology, photography—supplemented by our mother's library. Already obsessed with fishing, Brian became an expert on game fish, able to recite the state record for each species, the location of the catch, and the type of fly the fish bit on. Combined with experience, the insights into ethics, tactics, casting, fly-tying, knots, and aquatic insects he gleaned from guidebooks turned him into a master fisherman with aspirations of becoming a professional guide in Alaska.

Mountains intrigued me more than fish, so my mother introduced me to Ann Zwinger, who in *Land above the Trees* and *Beyond the Aspen Grove* managed through her descriptions of the flora, fauna, and topography of Colorado to fuse science and poetry. Her books revealed both how much and how little I knew about the beloved land I wandered, refocusing my eyes from the grander sweep to the finer points my mother had tried for so long to get me to see. I often passed orange and red lichens in boulder fields, but I had not known to thank the resident pikas and marmots for the sight until Zwinger taught me that "Rock plus nitrate from animal urine equals this brilliant lichen..." (*Land*, 63). She taught me about dragonfly nymphs, the voracious larvae that terrorize tadpoles and fairy shrimp in ponds. She taught me about *krummholz*, or "elfin timber" (58), waist-high thickets just below timberline that I first experienced during a family trip to the Snowy Range. My siblings and I walked atop the krummholz for long distances, enchanted by the feeling of having springs on our feet. As Zwinger taught me, we should have gone around rather than tread on these tiny trees that, left to grow, can live a thousand years. By leading us to books, our mother was perhaps weaning us, offering us other mentors, showing us how to find our own way to knowledge.

I took these lessons to heart. Over the years, I had become an environmentalist, a process that began in Perry Park and intensified during three summers I spent, as a college student, hauling trash and picking up litter along Rocky Mountain National Park's Trail Ridge Road. In my twenties, I quit a job as a newspaper editor in Wyoming and moved to Durango, Colorado, to work on a novel loosely based on my national park experiences. My parents made their disapproval clear when I quit a job to chase a dream. During the Depression, my mother often had to eat the squirrels her father shot in Topeka parks and my father recalled the horrors of mass bankruptcy, so they valued ambition and steady employment more than dreams. In fact, after living in Colorado for twenty years, they traded the paradise of Perry Park for the lure of better pay and a promotion in Texas.

Having also left Colorado for the more pristine landscape in Montana, I was teaching part-time in Bozeman when my wife gave birth to our first son. As a couple, my wife and I had spent ten years back-packing, canyon hiking, skiing, and mountain biking together before deciding to start a family, but neither of us quite understood the magnitude of this decision until Evan arrived. We had until then chosen to live in places of natural beauty even if doing so meant living a few millimeters above the poverty line. In *Between a Rock and a Hard Place*, Aron Ralston, a canyon hiker forced to amputate his right arm to save his life, describes this attitude, saying, "There's a mostly unspoken acknowledgment among the voluntarily impoverished dues-payers in our towns that it's better to be fiscally poor yet rich in experience—living the dream—than to be traditionally wealthy but live separate from one's passions" (11). We had vowed never to sell out, never to leave the mountains, but Evan's birth changed all that. In my own case, the sudden upsurge of wonder and responsibility as he and I first looked into each other's eyes pushed the reset button on my life, turned the Bridger Mountains into a backdrop, and made earning a living more important, by far, than a sense of place. As we admitted, "We can't eat the scenery—or feed it to the baby." The best job offer took us to Fort Worth, Texas. Among other benefits, the pay raise meant we could trade our pickup for a Toyota station wagon with room enough for a car seat.

Though I liked having a set of grandparents close by, I felt the absence of mountains as a palpable ache. Seeing the Dallas-Fort Worth "Metroplex" as a wasteland of malls, churches, and football stadiums, I insisted we take our tiny family west at every break in the school year. Only when the money ran thin did I open my eyes to the country surrounding Fort Worth. My mother began this process by pointing out the fields of bluebonnets and Indian blankets that undulated along the highways each spring. When I spoke wistfully of Bozeman and Perry Park, she said, "Anyone can love Montana and Colorado. Texas is harder to love because to see the good stuff you have to get closer to the ground." Sensing my resistance, she added, "When you're a parent, you do what you have to do for your children. And you make the most of where you find yourself."

She taught this "bloom where you're planted" mindset by example, throwing herself into volunteer work, gardening, and a systematic study of Texas literature, politics, and natural history. Though they spent time with their grandson, my parents also took frequent trips to the Hill Country, the Big Thicket, Big Bend, and other scenic places the guidebooks recommended. From the eaves of their home in Irving, thirty miles from Fort Worth, my mother hung nectar to attract hummingbirds. In their oak-shaded backyard stood feeders whose sunflower seeds drew not only songbirds but also raccoons and possums.

True to form, to help me adjust to life in Texas, my mother recommended books. One was John Graves's *Goodbye to a River*. Graves wrote so eloquently about the Brazos that I had to see it. I kayaked stretches below Possum Kingdom Lake, finding there a beautiful, though not pristine, river that cut through limestone hills and sustained such species as kingfishers, freshwater oysters, and alligator gar. Deer, coyotes, foxes, and feral hogs also ranged the river basin.

These discoveries took some of the sting out of being a flatlander. I longed to raise my children in the Rockies—to give them the freedom and love of nature my parents had given me—but the birth of our second son Scott, the family's first native Texan, would mean living in Fort Worth for the long haul. Texas was good to my parents, who saved enough to anticipate a comfortable retirement and avoid, as they said, "burdening our children." On a lesser scale, Texas gave me a career and my first house. Over the years, I also found a few wild patches of Texas, Arkansas, and Oklahoma in which to pass on to my sons the rugged lessons I'd learned as a boy, but I remained discontented. Animated debates with my mother helped me to see my longing for the Rockies as less about geography than about reclaiming my youth. Trips to Colorado confirmed that the Perry Park I knew no longer existed. Neither did the Rocky Mountain National Park of my college days. Seeking paradise, "native" Coloradans from California, Pennsylvania, Minnesota, Texas, Ohio, and Indiana had overrun the Front Range, building a metroplex that stretched from Pueblo to Fort Collins. As in Texas, nature in Colorado now existed in patches, though the patches were still big. I could uproot my family and maybe find a decent job in Denver, my mother said, but I could never go back to the Colorado I knew.

By the time Evan and Scott were old enough to have an opinion, they also had a strong sense of Fort Worth as home. One year, I applied for a job at Fort Lewis College in Durango and raised the possibility of moving there, hoping the boys would share my excitement. Instead, Evan's lower lip trembled and he said, "I wouldn't want to leave Texas."

My parents felt no such compunction. Having helped us to embrace life in the flats, they retired to Oregon for a second shot at childhood—a time of freedom, fun, and discovery in a place of natural beauty.

In keeping with her philosophy, when cancer cut this time short, my mother made the most of her final days. On our last visit, she knelt beside her grandsons on the state park beach near her new home to point out starfish, sea otters, crabs, and sand dollars, and to admire the strange objects her grandsons brought her. She followed along as they climbed boulders, walked atop driftwood logs as thick as redwoods, played chicken with the surf, and watched pelicans dive. At Jedediah Smith Redwoods State Park, she wandered among the immortals, identified the banana slugs Scott found, and held the boys' hands in attempts to encircle the largest trunks until, out of energy, she retired to the shade to watch them skip stones.

On our way out of the park, we passed a fallen redwood with a number of saplings—no more than eight inches wide but already tall—growing from its moldering trunk. In the backseat, my mother sat between the boys. I glanced back at her lined face, framed by the fresher faces of her grandsons, the family resemblance strong, and understood her final lesson. To this day, I'm not sure she was right, but if at the end of life we simply die and return to the earth the molecules that compose our bodies, if there is no afterlife beyond the memories and DNA we bequeath to those who loved us, then her children and grandchildren really are her offshoots, her chance at immortality.

To keep memories of her fresh, I sometimes leaf through *A Field Guide to Rocky Mountain Wildflowers*. When I think of her now, a dozen years after her death, I think of columbines and alpine primroses and pasqueflowers. I think of ruby-throated hummingbirds. I think of the landscapes she once wandered: the meadows, the sandstone cliffs, and the High Road into the mountains above Perry Park. I think of the delight she found in the places she lived, which she passed on to us. I think of my sons. I think of redwoods.

Works Cited

Craighead, John J., Frank C. Craighead, Jr., and Ray J. Davis. *A Field Guide to Rocky Mountain Wildflowers*. The Peterson Field Guide Series. Boston: Houghton Mifflin, 1963. Print.

Graves, John. *Goodbye to a River: A Narrative*. New York: Knopf, 1960. Print.

Ralston, Aron. *Between a Rock and a Hard Place*. New York: Atria. 2004. Print.

Zwinger, Ann. *Beyond the Aspen Grove*. New York: Random House, 1970. Print.

Zwinger, Ann H., and Beatrice E. Willard. *Land Above the Trees: A Guide to American Alpine Tundra*. New York: Harper & Row, 1972. Print.

Physical Education

With a flick of his thick wrist, Coach taught me to pay attention and drew the year's first blood.

The volleyball rebounded from my face and into his hands as if he had bounced it off a wall. I wiped blood from the corner of my mouth and blinked hard a few times. A moment later, as if to let me know it was nothing personal, Coach flung the ball into the nose of another unwary freshman.

In our high school, the term *physical education* carried several meanings. It meant the normal lessons we learned in the gymnasium from Coach, but it also meant the harsher lessons learned from classmates in the confines of the locker room or behind the gym after school. These lessons had links, forged and reinforced by the school's color-coded taxonomy of male P.E. students. Feats of strength, speed, and coordination determined whether each of us would receive white, red, blue, or gold shorts.

White shorts went to boys who lacked the muscular development to climb a rope forty feet to the gym ceiling, to climb a pegboard, to run a mile in under seven minutes, to run one hundred yards in under fourteen seconds, or to do a respectable number of push-ups, pull-ups, sit-ups, or bar dips.

Red shorts were a step above white, going to boys with average builds and some athletic skills.

Blue shorts went to boys, usually varsity athletes, with impressive wads of useful muscle and tufts of facial hair, who could climb a rope with their arms alone and speed along the track.

Gold shorts went to those rare creatures—two in the school's history—who set the standard for the rest, the demigods and superheroes of the football field and basketball court. Of the thirty boys in our ninth-grade P.E. class, two earned blue shorts, twenty earned red, and eight earned white.

A brief description of my physique that year will make obvious the color of shorts I wore. At age fourteen, I had hair on my head but nowhere else that counted. I had the apple-cheeked complexion of a preschooler, and adults often told my parents what a nice, cute, apple-cheeked boy they had. Some of the girls I liked also thought I was cute and nice in an apple-cheeked sort of way, and they continued to think of me in this way years later, long after I developed muscles and facial hair.

At five feet four inches tall and weighing in at 125 pounds, I started my freshman year as a victim. Bullies took one look at my round face and my gleaming mouthful of orthodontia and demanded my lunch money. I hated to give in without a fight, but my resistance did not change the outcome—empty pockets and lips cut ragged on my expensive braces.

So I ate lunch in the library, where during 40-minute increments I read William Hickling Prescott's 1,300-page opus *History of the Conquest of Mexico, History of the Conquest of Peru*. It's true I had an interest in New World history, but I had a greater interest in avoiding the daily muggings.

There was no avoiding physical education entirely, though.

For the first two weeks of P.E., while we took Coach's battery of fitness tests to determine the color of shorts we would wear, the strongest boys practiced an equal-opportunity brand of bullying. They picked on anyone who would take it. One budding felon, a football player named Rick, kept a supply of Baggies in his locker. Each day, instead of visiting a urinal, he simply urinated in a Baggie, closed it, and hurled it over the adjacent lockers. Rick was a junior varsity linebacker, who could climb the rope to the gym ceiling with only his arms, so he had nothing to fear from the boys at surrounding lockers—any one of whom would take a Baggie in the face sooner than take him on. We dressed fast, eyes cast upward, ready to evade his missiles. But each day someone would look away in time to get a drenching and suffer the laughter of those lucky enough to be dry.

The fitness tests went well for most of the boys in the class, even some of Rick's victims, but less well for a few of us. Desperate to win red shorts, I did the required number of pushups, bar dips, and sit-ups. I ran the hundred in under fourteen seconds. With a surge of strength fed by a fear of falling, and relying on the use of my legs, I climbed the rope. Unfortunately, I ran the mile in a little under eight minutes and managed only four of the ten required pull-ups. The pegboard—an eight-foot-tall, three-foot-wide torture device—was bolted to one wall of the gym, its lower end just out of the reach of my fingers. As Coach explained, to earn a pair of blue shorts, we had to climb the board by jamming large wooden pegs, held in our fists, into the holes and make our way to the top through a series of one-handed pull-ups. When it was my turn to try, I dangled from the first peg for as long as I could, straining to place the second in a higher hole, before accepting defeat.

The morning our shorts arrived, Coach singled out two of our classmates—Rick and a varsity wrestler named Ian—for special recognition. They stood before him like Medal of Honor winners, heads high, shoulders back, to accept a pair of blue shorts and anointment as class leaders. Coach tossed most of the other boys, who passed everything but the pegboard, pairs of red shorts, which they snatched out of the air with expressions of relief and pride. Then I and seven others—faces flushed, lips trembling, eyes cast down—took our white shorts like the beating Coach meant them to be.

Of average height but lean and muscular, Coach had large and hairy forearms, a square jaw, and an unshakeable self-assurance. "Some of you have work to do." He let his stern gray eyes rest briefly on mine. "If you don't like the shorts you're wearing, get motivated."

As he suggested, only a loser, a wimp, a lost cause, someone destined never to achieve manhood would suffer the indignity of white shorts without doing whatever he could to get stronger, faster, and tougher. The system sounded simple and fair, but it made no allowances for late bloomers or boys with abnormal physiques.

The color-coded shorts set the pecking order that would no doubt have formed even without Coach's help. Our school was, after all, located on the grounds of the United States Air Force Academy and blended the children of civilians, like me, with those of noncoms and officers who literally whipped their sons and daughters into shape.

A quick look at my white-shorted cohorts told me I was the only varsity athlete among them.

Yep, a varsity athlete.

A state-ranked tennis player, I had during summer tryouts beaten all but two seniors to become the team's third singles player. I had a sizzling serve, quick reflexes, and a fierce determination to win. But my triumphs on the court meant little to the blue- and red-shorted boys, or even to Coach, who had let slip that he saw tennis as equivalent to softball or field hockey.

Our common status should have united the wimps in white shorts, if only for mutual protection. Instead, we shunned each other, preferring to suffer alone. This attitude became clear to me one day when I tried to befriend a boy named Philip. In response to my greeting, he glanced away and muttered, "Don't talk to me, man."

Maybe Philip meant, like me, to somehow pass the next round of fitness tests and cross to the refuge of red shorts. I figured I could lower my mile time and eventually manage the ten pull-ups. Until then, we ran a gauntlet of boys whose colored shorts signified physical superiority. Even some of those who won red shorts by the smallest margin now felt free to shove, kick, or otherwise humiliate us. Three boys in particular took to heart their role as tormentors of the unfit. The ringleader, Jerry, looked like a blond coyote, with a rangy build, shifty eyes, and a prominent Adam's apple. As if he fed on his victims' emotions, he showed only a casual interest in the physical side of bullying, often culling the victims and then standing back to watch his followers work. Of these followers, Arturo, a Latino with a nascent mustache and a sullen expression, had the most dangerous reputation since the school had recently suspended his sister for pulling a knife on another girl. The other, Don, had curly blond hair and a pleasant-looking face which rage transformed into a scarlet mask that spewed spit, threats, and profanities. He often bragged that he'd broken every bone in his body except his nose, "and my old man says someone's bound to break it before I'm sixteen."

No one was likely to break Don's nose during P.E. Coach had banned fighting and threatened to flunk any offenders, but he stayed out of the locker room and tended to ignore any incident that did not become a full-blown fistfight. The ban only kept boys who cared about their grade from defending themselves. Jerry, Arturo, and Don revealed this sad fact one morning during a floor hockey game. Surrounding me, they jabbed their sticks into my ribs and laughed when I reminded them we might all flunk if we fought.

Arturo swung his stick into my left shin. "We're already flunking, ass-wipe."

Unwilling to tell my father what was happening at school, I covered up or explained away the worst of the bruises. An attorney and a decorated veteran of World War II, made kinder and gentler by combat, my father had long urged my younger brother and me to embrace pacifism. "There's never a good reason to fight," he said often. Neither of us entirely bought his argument, and I began pleading a case of my own for judo or karate lessons. If forced to fight, I wanted to fight well.

While I worked on my father, I took some consolation from watching Ian, the blue-shorted wrestler, assume the role of alpha male—and in the process beat, torque, or terrorize into submission Jerry, Arturo, Don, and even Rick the linebacker. A second-year freshman, Ian had a reputation for psychopathic violence that began in middle school. In a shop class, he had over a nine-week period needled and harassed another boy to the breaking point. The boy, Patrick, picked up a nearby hammer and twice bounced it off Ian's head before Ian battered him. The school suspended them both, and Patrick's parents moved him to another district. Now Ian—a borderline albino with pale blue eyes and an acne-scarred face—made a decent living extorting lunch money from boys who had not yet discovered the library.

As alpha male, he focused his flat, pale gaze on potential usurpers and left the white-shorted boys alone. We were invisible, beneath his notice—until my mother washed my gym shorts with a pair of red ski socks. The shorts came out a shade of pink so subtle I didn't detect the dye job until I lined up beside another boy in white shorts. Jerry pointed me out to Ian. They stood together for a while, as if Ian needed time to comprehend what he was seeing. Then they came over for a closer look.

Ian's insolent smile and penetrating stare had frozen the blood of more than one boy in our class and froze mine now. He flicked his eyes down and back up to my face, as if assessing my apple cheeks and braces in the new light of my pink shorts. Under Ian's gaze, my fear and humiliation slowly turned into anger. And as if he sensed the change in me, he took a quick step forward, crouching slightly, hands raised as if for grappling. That's when Coach came into the gym and told us to line up for calisthenics. Ian shook his head slowly, as if in disgust at the poor timing, and pointed a thick finger at me.

I skipped the shower after P.E. and developed a bad case of Ian-itis that kept me out of school for two days. My mother frowned in concern each morning when I complained of a gut ache, and she asked in various ways if I were having trouble at school. On the second day, she found my shorts in the laundry room, soaking in a vat of Clorox, and confronted me with the evidence. In the end, I told her most of the story, including Ian's implied threat.

"You know you can't hide at home for the rest of your life," she said. "Sooner or later, you'll have to stand up for yourself."

"Even if that means I have to fight?"

She surprised me by shrugging. "If it comes to that."

That night, my father came into my room to talk about the importance of facing one's fears head-on. He made no reference to Ian but spoke of Mahatma Gandhi's nonviolent resistance to the oppression of the British Empire and Martin Luther King Junior's nonviolent resistance to racism in America.

"They found ways to resolve their problems without fighting," he said, "and they stuck to their principles no matter the cost. It's something I want you to think about."

Like my father, I admired both men for their willingness to die for a cause, but at fourteen my chief cause was surviving to fifteen. And I had already tried turning the other cheek. My father's circumspection meant I did not have to spell all this out to him. At the end of his speech, he patted my knee and said, "I want you to go back to school tomorrow. I have every confidence you can face your fears and resolve your problems peacefully."

At school the next day, everyone I passed in the halls looked at me as if they saw the coward within.

In P.E., this sensation had greater force, only I was not imagining it. Instead of taking my beating like a man, I had run home to hide. So I stood now at the absolute bottom of the pecking order, once again beneath the notice of Ian, who for several days left me to the gentler fists, elbows, knees, and hockey sticks of Jerry, Arturo, Don, and the lesser bullies.

Maybe it was the open contempt of the other white-shorted boys; maybe it was my mother's urging me to stand up for myself. Whatever the reason, when a notorious towel popper—Doug—left a welt on my upper thigh after my shower one day, I popped him back with the speed and hand-eye coordination gained from years of net play. Tall and chunky, Doug had a curly red 'fro, pale freckled skin, a nasally voice, and teeth so big he seldom closed his mouth. He let out squeals of pain as I traded him welt for welt. Then he turned and scuttled for his locker.

Doug's retreat was my first victory and served notice to the others that I would no longer run home to hide. It gave me a dose of overconfidence that led, a few days later, to trouble with Jerry, Arturo, and Don. The trio had pinned me against the gymnasium's folding bleachers. Jerry looked on while Arturo and Don gave me the usual lighthearted pounding and added a few more bruises to my collection. To get Don to back off, I feigned a punch toward his perfect nose. To the surprise of everyone in the class, including me, the punch landed.

It wasn't much as punches go, but it sent Don stumbling backward. Though still intact, his nose trickled blood. Tears welled in his savage eyes.

Jerry and Arturo looked at me, their own eyes somber and their mouths hanging open. Don started toward me, his face scarlet. Coach arrived then to break things up and to send me on my first trip to the vice principal's office.

A large wooden paddle—its lacquer stained and flecked—hung like a trophy above the desk. The vice principal looked at Coach's detention slip and across at me, puzzlement and irritation on his wide, ruddy face. He pressed the intercom button and asked the school secretary to deliver my file, which he scanned. "Your grades are good. You haven't been in trouble before, or I'd know you. What the hell's your problem?"

I explained the situation with Jerry, Arturo, and Don. "I guess I'm tired of getting hit."

"So you hit back."

"Sort of by accident," I reminded him.

He glanced over his shoulder at the paddle. "No more accidents. Understand?" He waited for me to nod. "I'm giving you a week's lunch detention in the study hall, starting today."

The study hall had two rows of tables and chairs, roughly half of them occupied by the school's delinquents. Arturo's sister Angela, back from her suspension, was among them. So was Ian, who greeted my arrival with a blood-chilling stare. I sat at the other table, across from Dorn, my lab partner in biology. Over six feet tall, African American, and the first cousin of a football player tough enough to routinely hijack from Ian the lunch money Ian hijacked from boys like me, Dorn could not bring himself even to touch a frog. So when assigned to dissect one, I did all the cutting while he took the notes. We had been friends ever since. At lunch and between classes, he often stood in the hall at his cousin's toll station, and thanks to our friendship I had a free pass. We smiled at each other across the table and he raised his eyebrows as if to ask what I was doing there. I couldn't tell him because the study hall monitor, Mr. Johnson, had recited the rules at the door: No eating, no drinking, no gum chewing, no talking without permission. "Read a book," he said. "Get some homework done."

So I opened my biology text and, to amuse Dorn, pretended to speed-read it, scanning pages almost as fast as I could turn them. During the first week of biology, I had pretended to do the same thing before a chapter quiz. "You're shittin' me," he said. "No one can read that fast."

Dorn had quizzed me, and I'd answered all the questions right. In the end, I admitted, "Okay, I'm shitting you. I read it last night."

Not so funny the first time, the joke gave Dorn a case of the giggle-snorts today and earned us a scowl from Mr. Johnson. The next day, in P.E., I learned that we had also caught the attention of Ian. As he approached me before class, I thought the time had come for a reckoning. Instead, he asked, "Can you teach me how to speed-read?"

His acne-scarred face bore an earnest expression almost as terrifying as his psychopathic stare.

"I don't know," I said.

I did not know if I could teach Ian how to speed-read because I did not know how to speed-read. To avoid a beating, I suggested we start the lessons in detention the next day, giving me time to find a book on the subject. That night I bought *Triple Your Reading Speed* by Wade Cutler and read it as fast as I could.

Mr. Johnson smiled when I asked if I could tutor Ian during detention. He even ushered the other delinquents, including Dorn, to the far side of the room to give us some space. Ian actually read pretty well. Until then, I thought, "How hard can it be to triple his reading speed if he reads twenty words a minute?" According to the diagnostic test in the book, he actually read about two hundred words a minute with slightly below average comprehension. That day we worked on scanning clusters of words rather than one word at a time, and by the end of the first tutorial, his speed and comprehension had increased. Even so, he frowned. "As fast as you read the other day," he said. "That's what I want to do."

"First, you have to learn to scan clusters of words, then sentences, then paragraphs, then pages." I almost compared the challenge to learning a topspin backhand. Instead, I said, "It's like learning to do a takedown, only harder. You have to do it in steps." And I would have to learn the steps before I could teach him.

Ian gave a grudging nod, and my prospects for surviving to fifteen looked good until Arturo's sister Angela said, "Dummy can't read."

Most of the delinquents laughed. Dorn didn't. Neither did Mr. Johnson, who rewarded Angela with another week's detention. Ian froze in his chair, his thick neck bent in shame. With a sudden movement, he swept the Cutler book off the table and turned his flat gaze on me.

The reckoning came after school the next day. As I hurried toward the varsity locker room to dress for tennis, I had the usual load of books clamped under my arm. Ian crept up behind me and punched the books, scattering them across the hardwood floor of the gym. Among them was

Cutler's *Triple Your Reading Speed*. Crouching, hands up, he circled to block my way to the locker room.

"Pick 'em up," I said.

His mouth fell open and his pale eyes widened for an instant. I shared his disbelief but could not take back the words. He swung his fist in a looping punch that should have put me out. By reflex, I rolled my head at the instant his fist struck my chin and mouth. The blow rocked me. The world flickered. I tasted blood. The teeth in my lower left jaw felt loose but stayed put thanks to the braces. My knees wobbled but did not collapse.

I glared at Ian, chin thrust out. "Now you can pick 'em up."

What he did next rocked me as hard as the punch. His acne-scarred face drew down in a look of regret, and he bent to gather the books. He handed them to me. "I'm sorry," he said.

In biology the next day, Dorn made a face at my swollen jaw. A football player had watched me, the tennis player who wore pink shorts in P.E., take Ian's knock-out punch without going down, Dorn said. The witness also saw Ian pick up and hand back my books.

I had no answers for Dorn's questions—spoken or unspoken. I could not explain why Ian had not battered my face or broken my elbows. Like the eye-witness, maybe he believed he had given me his best shot. Maybe he wasn't the psycho everyone thought. Maybe he had a streak of decency in him. Or maybe he still hoped to become a speed-reader and realized, after his first punch, the foolishness of concussing his tutor.

My father liked this last interpretation—the idea that I'd averted a fight by using my brain. I had turned the other jaw and peace ensued. Whatever Ian's motives, and I never had the courage to ask him, the rumor of my having fought him and survived brought an immediate decline in the bullying. Each day in P.E., Ian nodded or greeted me by name, a gesture that for a while kept even Jerry, Arturo, and Don at bay.

The respite gave me time to grow. By sophomore year, I stood four inches taller and had gained twenty-five pounds of muscle, with which I earned my first pair of red shorts. Having crossed to safety, I did what I could for the underdeveloped or genetically unlucky bastards in white. These boys would someday mature, lose or gain weight, develop muscles and facial hair, grow into men. The outrages heaped on them by those in blue or red shorts, or via the lessons delivered by Coach or other institutional bullies, would leave scars, some of them permanent. Not long ago, 73-year-old Carl Ericsson admitted to murdering a former classmate for putting a jockstrap on his head, a high school locker-room prank that occurred more than fifty years earlier. Ericsson rang the man's doorbell, confirmed his alleged former bully's identity, and shot him down (Lammers). Articles about this event convey puzzlement, as if the authors cannot fathom how Ericsson could harbor rage about this seemingly trivial event for so long a time. News articles more commonly recount the stories of sweet, sensitive souls who, unable to face their humiliation, have killed themselves instead of their tormentors. For example, Hibbard reports that Joel Morales, 12, hanged himself after bullies teased him about the death of his father. And Christian Boyle notes that Amanda Cummings, 15, jumped in front of a city bus after suffering intolerable bullying for having the temerity to date a boy on whom one of her victimizers had a crush. Such cases are, thankfully, relatively rare when one considers the magnitude of bullying that occurs in schools. Most victims do not embrace the darkness of revenge or suicide, though they may understand at least a part of what motivates those who do. Perhaps, like me, they have contemplated revenge without seeking it, electing instead to earn a black belt in Tae Kwon Do, join the Marine Corps, or pump more iron than Lou Ferrigno—determined never to be bullied again. Bruises fade and cuts heal, but the effects of bullying can last a lifetime.

Works Cited

Boyle, Christina. "Bullied Staten Island Teen Kills Self." *New York Daily News. com.* 3 Jan, 2012. Web.

Hibbard, Laura. "Joel Moralex, 12-Year-Old, Hangs Himself after School Bullies Tease Him about Dead Father. *The Huffington Post.* 31 May, 2012. Web.

Lammers, Dick. "Carl Ericsson Sentenced to Life in Prison for Murdering Norman Johnson over 1950s High School Prank." *The Huffington Post.* 27 Aug, 2012. Web.

Rumors of His Death

Dad sits up in bed, his lips twisted in a faded half smile as he looks at his children, who have rushed from Texas and California to see him for the last time.

"Listen to me, everyone. I have some final instructions. When I'm gone, I want you to spread my body in equal portions over the state park beach in Brookings, the old homestead in Perry Park, and the Blue Spruce Campground in Colorado, where we used to go when you were kids." He pauses as if overcome with emotion. "And I don't want to be cremated."

I laugh, and he joins me, his laugh feeble. Already in mourning, eyes leaking tears, my three sisters stare at us.

"On the way here," I say, "I saw a shop that rents wood chippers."

He nods somberly. "That should do the job."

My older sister Janet stares at us. "You've never been funny, and you're even less funny now."

She's right, I guess. Hairy cell leukemia is no laughing matter, though the name always brings to mind the image of an old man with bushy eyebrows and hair sticking out of his ears—a fair description now of Dad. She's also wrong. When he isn't shy, or playing the tight-lipped attorney, or brooding over friends lost in the South Pacific, Dad can crack you up. Our mother used to say his wit got him through World War II, law school, forty years of tough cases, and a lifetime of social awkwardness. At the family dinner table, he often regaled us with stories of his life as the spoiled youngest son of a railroad station master in western Kansas and of his ongoing failures as a carpenter, car mechanic, fisherman, and practitioner of any other useful occupation. Though he twice argued before the Supreme Court, he chose law school only when the medical schools turned him down. "But I would have been a terrible doctor," he once confided. "I hate sick people."

He wasn't joking. As children, stricken by measles, mumps, strep, or chicken pox, we could go days without seeing him. Our mother would tend us—swollen and feverish—and pass along his best wishes. Now, he is sick to the point of death and no doubt filled with self-loathing.

To cheer him up, we take out the DVDs his grandchildren—all musicians—made for him. My nieces sing and play the piano. One of my sons, a gifted guitarist, plays and sings James Taylor's "Close Your Eyes." An audiophile, Dad has eclectic tastes in music that range from classical to classic rock. Partial to the Big Band jazz of the forties, he nevertheless introduced us in our early teens to the Beatles, the Stones, Carol King, and Jerry Reed. In his own teens, he was so consummate a clarinetist that the Navy Band recruited him, but instead he spent two years driving a Sherman tank in the Philippines and New Guinea, and after the war he abandoned dreams of directing the New York Philharmonic to pursue medicine and then law. After a hard day in court, and oiled by a few scotch and waters, he spent most evenings in front of the stereo, conducting Mozart, Beethoven, or Copeland, waving his arms in flamboyant rhythm, trilling his fingers to bring up the woodwinds, and stabbing a hand at the back of the orchestra to cue the cymbals. He might flash us a self-deprecating grin, but he fooled no one. He was serious about music. He passed this passion on to us, and each of us passed it on to our own children.

Toward the end of the visit, Dad is sleeping—mouth open, face pallid, irregular breaths coming in gasps. The oncologist stands a few feet away, flanked by a nurse and an intern. Tall and bearded, the doctor tells us how much he has enjoyed talking to our father about jazz. He answers our questions in a soothing tone that betrays, along its edges, a desire to placate us with a few careful words and get on with his rounds, on to patients who still have a chance. His smile comes and goes like a nervous tick, alternating with a look of compassion and steadfast concern.

"As I mentioned on the phone, the chemotherapy drug that was your father's best hope almost killed him outright—fever, sky-rocketing blood pressure, heart palpitations." He flashes us the smile, which melts into compassion and steadfast concern. "We almost lost him yesterday, and I don't expect him to live past tomorrow."

This prognosis brought us to Seattle, and later that afternoon it prompts my sisters and Miriam, Dad's girlfriend of ten years, to sort his things into piles—a large one to go to Goodwill and six smaller ones to divvy among us survivors, including our brother, who couldn't make the trip.

I stand off to the side and watch them go through Dad's clothes. Janet holds up a stack of folded boxers. "You want these?"

"Pass."

As the eldest child, she is the executor. "I'd hate to see them go to waste."

"Thanks, but I've been buying my own undies since I turned forty."

"Ha, ha," she says and thrusts the boxers into a trash bag.

Her rigid posture and cool gaze make me wonder if she is more upset about the wood chipper joke or about my intervention on behalf of our younger sisters, who met my plane and spent the ride from the airport to Miriam's house complaining about her condescending attitude. Ingrid said, "You need to talk to Janet. She calls me 'Baby' and Lisa 'Sweetie' in the most patronizing tone, like she thinks she's Mom. And she's been ordering us around."

Lisa agreed. "We told her to cut the shit, so she cried and asked why we didn't love her anymore. Of course we love her. We just want her to treat us like adults."

Dark-haired, clear-eyed, and pretty, they both look younger than they are—early forties—but no one would mistake them for babies. As soon as I could, I pulled Janet aside and told her what Ingrid and Lisa had said. Janet's wide, sensitive face went cold. Then the tears came.

"We're about to be orphaned, and now they don't love me anymore."

I rested a hand on her shoulder. "They're grown women, with families of their own. They don't want to be treated like kids."

"That's not how I mean it. 'Baby' and 'Sweetie' are terms of endearment."

"You wouldn't use terms like that at the office, right? Try treating them like colleagues—maybe call them by their names instead of by terms they don't find endearing."

Janet wiped her eyes. "It's a habit. I'm not sure I can stop myself."

A few minutes later, she asked Baby to go through Dad's bedroom closet and Sweetie to start with the sock drawer. Ingrid and Lisa shot me looks but did as Janet asked.

There are signs of Dad all over Miriam's house. In framed images of the pyramids of Giza and the Matterhorn, Dad looks tall and substantial, his longish white hair blowing in the wind. He and Miriam met on a Nile cruise four years after our mother's death, traded e-mails, and moved in together. Each had lost a spouse to cancer. Each brought to the merger enough assets to make marriage legally messy, so, as Dad explained, "We've decided to live in sin." In a veiled and appalling reference to their sex life, he let slip, shortly after he introduced me to Miriam, that she made him feel like a teenager again. "When your mother died, I never thought I'd find love again, but I have."

Petite and fit for her age, Miriam has a pleasant smile and kindly blue eyes. For ten years she has shared her well-appointed home and a series of Elder Hostel adventures with Dad. Even so, we warmed to her slowly. The first time he brought her to Fort Worth, she knelt beside my young sons and said, "You can call me Grandma." In the next beat, I told them, "You can call her Miriam." On a weekend visit to Ingrid's place in Topanga Canyon, Miriam took a Gray Panther's stance against babysitting and urged Dad to do the same. "We've raised our children," she said to explain their refusal to watch nine-month-old Sage while Ingrid picked up her husband from work. Ingrid woke Sage from a nap for the long, hot drive across Los Angeles. That night, she phoned to say, "Mom would have insisted on spending some time alone with her granddaughter."

Though Ingrid still bears a small grudge, we all learned to like Miriam during the past three years as she pulled Dad through the early stages of leukemia. Anyone who saw them together, laughing as they drank wine and played Scrabble, could see they loved each other.

To please her now, I obey her command to try on Dad's wardrobe of coats and jackets—expensive and fashionable for a man of eighty-three but not my style. Miriam insists each jacket looks good on me even though the sleeves end three inches above my wrists. In the end, I accept two fleece pullovers I can wear hiking or biking. She also offers me Dad's collection of shoes and hats. From them, I choose a felt hat Dad wore to the beach and a pair of Nike Airs he bought but never wore.

I stop in the middle of lacing the shoes and glance up at the four women. "What if the doctor's wrong? If Dad survives, he'll have nothing to wear home from the hospital."

A short silence ensues. Then they go back to sorting his things.

"Let's take a walk," Ingrid says.

Outside, the Puget Sound glitters in the distance as we stroll past homes built a decade earlier for a tenth of their current value. We are the creative siblings, the ones our family voted most likely to live in poverty— she an actress, who often lands minor roles in major movies, and I a former journalist, who teaches at a small college. The bond that carried us through family gatherings tells me that she has something important to say.

She slips an arm through mine. "Last night, Miriam said she can't take care of Dad even with a home-health nurse. If he goes into remission, he can't come home."

The news burrows into the base of my throat. "Has she told him?"

Ingrid blinks a pair of pale blue eyes that movie cameras adore for their size and expressiveness. "They picked out a hospice a few miles from here—close enough to make visiting easy. Dad asked Janet to clear out his things so Miriam doesn't have to. She's eighty. There's only so much she can do."

Knowing he has no home to return to makes his impending death real in a way the doctor's grim prognosis had not. "Well, goddamn it."

Ingrid smiles. "For a second, you sounded just like Dad at rush hour."

I look and sound like Dad, everyone says, but the one key trait he passed to me, by example not DNA, is road rage. As he once put it: "Everywhere I go, the highways are filled with sons of bitches." I mimic his tone of puzzled outrage as I quote him to Ingrid.

"But he's always so gentle in his anger," she says. "One time, in L.A., he tried to flip off another driver but couldn't quite bring himself to do it. He flashed him an index finger instead, like 'we're number one,' and the guy kept glancing over, unsure how to react."

We laugh as we make our way back to Miriam's house.

That night, we travel downtown as a group, but most of us will return to Miriam's house to sleep. Lisa will spend the night sitting up with Dad, and she carries a bag with enough snacks and Harlequin novels to get her through the ordeal. I plan to do the same tomorrow, taking a cab from the hospital directly to the airport for a Monday morning flight back to Texas.

Dad looks fragile. There's a haunted quality in his eyes, and when Ingrid asks how he feels, he falters. Janet opens an album of photographs from our childhood in Colorado. As she points to different pictures and reminisces about family picnics and camping trips, Dad's eyes slide away from the pages and up to our faces. Ingrid and Lisa weep openly. I'm trying to think of something to lighten the mood, but nothing comes to me. Fond of Mark Twain's quip "Rumors of my death have been greatly exaggerated," Dad has spent much of his adult life poking fun at the idea of dying. Now he's up against it, and the humor has left him—left us all.

He shuts his eyes and sinks into his pillows. "I'm sorry, kids. I'm having a rough time tonight."

We understand, we say, and will see him tomorrow. In the hallway, my sisters muffle their sobs in each other's shoulders. Outside the huddle, I pat the random back.

We're up early the next morning, loading trash bags into Ingrid's rental car, Dad's Acura, and Miriam's Volvo. Our caravan makes its way to a suburban Goodwill store so new it shines even in the muted winter sunlight.

Fifteen minutes later, Dad is wearing the only clothes he owns. The homeless, the destitute, and the bargain hunters of Seattle will soon inherit his coats, shirts, pants, hats, shoes, socks, and boxers. They'll also get their pick of watches, Swiss Army knives, and other gadgets he compulsively bought on the Internet. By noon, and for pennies on the dollar, Half-Price has acquired his books, movies, and compact disks. Everything else that Miriam does not want is in moving boxes or arranged in neat stacks.

While Miriam spends the afternoon at the hospital, we convene at a local pancake house. For a couple of hours, we talk about work, husbands and wives, kids, our absent brother—anything but our father. Then Ingrid says, "Listen, I've been thinking that maybe we shouldn't cry in front of Dad. I can see it bothers him."

I've been thinking along the same lines. "Crying only reminds him he's two steps from death. We need to treat him like he's still among the living."

Janet and Lisa look at us as if we've slapped them. Janet asks, "Why wouldn't we cry when we're about to lose the man who took care of us all our lives? I'm sure Daddy understands even if you don't."

Ingrid and I find each other's eyes. "Daddy" rings false. So does the image of a lifelong caretaker. An old-fashioned man, Dad has always been a softer touch to his daughters than his sons, but above all he values self-reliance. He weaned my brother and me early, financially speaking, making clear that our success or failure in life hinged on our education, talent, and drive. We had his love, he said. As long as we supported ourselves, did not look to him for handouts, we would also have his respect. Ingrid weaned herself. At twenty-one, she was earning enough as a court reporter to move to L.A. and pursue an acting career on the side—against Dad's advice. Janet and Lisa had a harder time cutting the ties, leaving home for good in their late twenties. Over the years, I have come to see our father, with all his faults, as a close and dear friend. I admire him, but I don't idolize him.

Ingrid tries again: "All I'm saying is we should try to make his last days happy ones."

Janet brushes away an angry tear. "You cope in your way and let us cope in ours. You have no right to tell us how to grieve or how to act when we're with Daddy."

Her gaze flat and cool, Ingrid dismisses this declaration with a shrug, but I'm thinking Janet is right: none of us has a special insight into managing grief or helping Dad prepare to die. Thanks to variables of gender, birth order, personality, and experience, each of us knows a different Dad—or Daddy—so we can't take a common approach to his death or our grief.

The waitress arrives with the check. We reach for wallets or purses, eager to back away from the standoff.

That evening, my sisters get through an entire hospital visit without crying—until we're in the hall, hugging goodbye. We won't see each other again until we spread Dad's ashes around his favorite places in Colorado and Oregon.

Back in the room, he has his eyes closed as if he's sleeping, but when I sit in the chair next to the bed, he reaches over and takes my hand.

"You okay?" I ask.

He hesitates. "I guess I'm afraid one of these times I'll close my eyes and never wake up."

At age eighty-five, my grandfather lay down on a couch to read, fell asleep, and died. My aunt found him in apparent slumber, *King Lear* lying open across his chest, so Dad's fears are justified. "You probably don't want me to fetch you a copy of Shakespeare's collected works?"

He gives me a feeble laugh. "No thanks."

"What can I do for you?"

Suddenly shy, he asks, "Would you rub my feet?"

For the first time since I came to Seattle, I have to fight an aching, almost overpowering urge to cry. When I was a kid, eight or nine years old, he used to have me rub his feet after a hard day at work. This act became one of my chores, like cutting firewood in the winter or mowing the grass in the summer. It takes me a moment to answer. "Sure."

His feet are flabby and look smaller than I remember. So do his legs. Leukemia has consumed this man, once tall and strong, and left only bone, fat, and tendon. I rub his feet gently, trying not to press too hard.

"Maybe Janet told you, but I'm not leaving much to you kids. If I have a regret, that's it. I meant to leave more behind, but between traveling and this goddamned leukemia, I've gone through my savings. There may be enough to help out with college tuition for the grandkids, but it's not going to change anyone's life."

I mutter reassurances. No doubt we could all use more money, but none of us needs it.

He sighs and takes several breaths. "Listen, I know you were closer to your mother than to me, and I was hard on you when you were a kid, but I want you to know while there's still time that I've always been proud that you and Ingrid had the guts to do what you wanted with your lives. I never had that kind of courage. If I had, you'd be looking at a retired orchestra leader instead of a broken-down old lawyer."

Part of me wants to offer comfort by denying the truth of this admission, but I can't. His words of regret about failing to pursue the big dream affected Ingrid and me, as children and as adults, in ways he never intended. "Thanks, Dad, it means a lot."

"And I always wished we could be closer."

My mother liked to talk and doled out generous doses of sympathy, support, and life-lessons.. Dad might tell funny stories at family gatherings, but he wasn't much for conversation, especially about puberty, sexuality, or self-doubt. And he didn't like looking at us during those rare times when he did agree to talk. He and I did our serious talking in the car, at night, staring straight ahead at the road. He seldom volunteered advice —I had to ask for it—but he delivered it in so thoughtful and circumspect a manner that when he did speak, I usually listened. Even as an adult, I often consulted him about the big decisions—marriage, divorce, career moves—seeking not approval but a calm, well-considered opinion.

"Yeah," I say, "growing up, I felt a little closer to Mom, but when I needed to talk about something important, who did I come to?"

Enough said. He closes his eyes and lets his head fall back on his pillow. I tuck a blanket around his feet and go into the hall. At the nursing station sits a woman in orange scrubs with soft, tired eyes and stress lines around her mouth. "Uh, that's my dad in the last room on the left. The doctor says he's probably going to die tonight, and I was wondering what to do when the time comes."

The soft, tired eyes stare at me for a moment. "What's his name?"

When I tell her, she studies his chart and shakes her head. "Dying tonight with those vital signs? Listen, Jack, that man's not going to die tonight or anytime soon—maybe not for weeks or months."

"But the doctor—"

She rolls her eyes. "Doctors!"

"Are you sure?"

"I work with terminal patients four nights a week, and their vitals don't look anything like your father's. He's dying but not for a while yet."

A damp February snow falls on the streets outside the hospital. Dad's hand is cool and dry in my grasp. "I talked to the nurse. Your vital signs are strong. She says there's no way you're going to die tonight."

"She said that?"

His rasping voice conveys surprise, not pleasure, at the prospect of living another day. Then he smiles. "So rumors of my death have been slightly exaggerated."

"That's right. Looks like I should plan another trip to Seattle."

"No," he says. "I don't want you kids to see me any worse than I am now. We've had a good visit and said goodbye. That's enough."

A short time later, he falls into the deepest sleep of the night. I go back to a plastic chair near the window to watch the snow. I wonder what he'll do when he finds out we've donated all his clothing to Goodwill. Maybe he'll laugh. Maybe he won't. To soften the blow, I take his felt beach hat and one of the fleece pullovers from my suitcase and hang them in his closet, wishing now that I'd accepted his boxers and a pair of pants so he could have a complete outfit.

At dawn, he's still sleeping. I whisper goodbye, kiss his forehead for the last time, and head out into the snow to catch a cab for the airport. Later in the week, Janet will rent a small truck and a car trailer to haul his worldly possessions to Texas. Her husband will fly up to make the drive with her. If Dad lives for weeks or months longer, she will return then to settle his affairs. When the moment comes, the Neptune Society will collect his body, cremate it, and deliver the ashes. Everything's ready. All that's left is to wait for Dad to die.

In the Footsteps of Captain Filth

The orange light of dawn tinted the peaks of the Never Summer Range and a red-winged blackbird sang from the marshes along the Colorado River. By eight, the rangers would report for work. By ten, the Winnebagos would be bumper to bumper on Trail Ridge Road, Rocky Mountain National Park's high-altitude scenic ramble. I would have liked to spend the intervening hours enjoying the quiet beauty of the morning.

But duty called.

I stopped the pickup and trash slid forward in the bed. In our endless search for litter, my partner Leroy and I expected to find Coors cans, three-pound Pampers, and the occasional road-killed elk. But today our headlights illuminated a plush, red, faux-leather chair and a matching hassock, which together blocked half the road and managed to surprise even us.

"What kind of asshole—?" Leroy sputtered.

I shrugged, and we got out of the truck to toss part of somebody's living room into the trash bin.

Being a park garbage man had never been my ambition.

I loved the outdoors and had no desire to see its seedy side, naively assuming when chosen from among thousands of applicants for a National Park Service position that I would spend my time building trails or giving campfire talks. I wanted to be a park ranger—that best liked of public officials, Boy Scout and Canadian Mounty rolled up in one—and felt sure someone had made a mistake when, upon my arrival at park headquarters, the head clerk directed me to Maintenance Superintendent Spud Tyler, my new boss, who issued me a large box of trash can liners.

There I learned I was replacing a man nicknamed Captain Filth. Though we never met, I soon discovered this bearded figure was the Paul Bunyon of trash in Rocky Mountain. If one could believe the old-timers, Captain Filth was a maintenance man par excellence, who hauled more trash and dug more interesting artifacts out of the garbage than anyone in the park's history. They made it clear that Leroy and I could never hope to fill Captain Filth's shoes.

Still, for three summers beginning in 1976 we roamed the park's roads, emptying trash barrels and disposing of beer cans, Pampers, faux-leather chairs, and unsightly road kills in a territory that stretched from the banks of the Colorado River's north fork to the high mountain tundra at Fall River Pass.

For the first few weeks, proud of our gray and green uniforms, we played at being rangers, going out of our way to help stranded motorists and referring to the garbage run as a patrol. Once, coming upon a long line of cars at the top of the pass, where an impenetrable fog had blinded the terrified drivers, we pulled around to the front and, with emergency lights flashing, led them to safety in the valley. Then we realized we were fooling no one—our lack of a gold badge and Smokey Bear hat was painfully obvious. The same people who worshipped the rangers, begging them to stand still for photographs, despised us when they noticed us at all.

Leroy and I became aware of this fact one morning at a scenic viewpoint overlooking the park's Kawuneeche Valley. A toddler standing a few feet away pointed at us and asked his mother who we were. "Nobody," she said, "just the morons who haul the trash."

Leroy, well on his way to a master's degree in international economics, took exception to this remark. I got him to return to the truck peaceably by giving him an Oreo cookie, for which he had an addiction, but the incident left scars.

For a time, we withdrew into ourselves, seeking comfort in the occasional illicit love letter that came to us through the trash. And there was some satisfaction in knowing the taxpayers paid us two dollars an hour more than the rangers, a fact we never failed to play up when a ranger passed our truck holding his nose. Then it dawned on us that there really were advantages, other than financial, to being trash collectors.

As drones, we were free of the sterling image the rangers had to carry around. We had no dignity to maintain, and as long as we kept the park clean and looked busy our bosses left us alone. Though seldom intentionally rude to park visitors, we could be flexible in responding to their questions. If a tourist asked, as one once did: "You keep the tundra looking so nice and neat—how often do you mow it?" a ranger would stifle his smile and explain that tundra grows this way in its natural state. We said, "Once a week."

Leroy once approached a woman whose children were feeding peanuts to the fat chipmunks gathered at a viewpoint and told her, "I wouldn't let your kids get too close, lady. We've had reports that some of the rodents here carry the bubonic plague."

She panicked, herding her children to the family camper and shouting orders to wash their hands.

"Won't help to wash," Leroy said, following along. "Plague's carried by fleas. Either they have it or they don't."

Oddly, Leroy was a bit of a hypochondriac, spending several hundred dollars on lab tests that summer to make sure he didn't have the plague himself. His fears stemmed from our constant contact with road kills—the hundreds of chipmunks, marmots, weasels, and snowshoe hares crushed under tourists' tires each summer. Spud had written their disposal into our job description, and in order to bear up under this hideous task we turned it into a ritualized sport.

Friends who in the same breath told us we would never break Captain Filth's record for throwing road kills insisted that our Road Kill Olympics, a series of contests to see who could fling a particular species the highest, farthest, and most accurately—using a short stick—was a thinly disguised attempt at concealing our disgust from ourselves and each other. They compared it to the pump truck operator's habit of eating chocolate pudding on days he pumped out the park's pit toilets.

Though we scoffed at such a notion, we wondered if they might be right one morning when we saw what at first appeared to be a medium-sized animal lying dead in the road. On closer inspection we discovered it was, in fact, a number of smaller ones lying together in a single heap.

A forensic examination suggested that a car had run over one of the animals, a Richardson's ground squirrel, while it attempted to cross the highway. A second ground squirrel had evidently gone out to feed on the body of the first and died under the wheels of yet another car—as had, one by one, at least half a dozen more ground squirrels.

"Here's your chance to catch up," Leroy said and checked the statistics we kept on a pad of paper in the glove box. A well-thrown road kill normally brought three points, with three more granted for style if the carcass passed within inches of a moving car. Leroy, whose deft flicks of the wrist could send a chipmunk spinning sixty feet off the road, was ahead by almost forty points and smug in his lead.

I found a stick at the roadside and approached the carcasses, surprised by a faint nausea. Having sent hundreds of small animals through make-believe goal posts over the years, I should have felt nothing at all.

"These are worth at least six points apiece," I told Leroy. "I think

I'm going to be sick."

"How many are there?"

I counted eight at first, then nine. With eyes averted, using the stick as a catapult, I began launching the ground squirrels off the road, going for speed and distance rather than style. Seven vanished over Trail Ridge Road's embankment before my technique gave out. I had overlooked a small spur at the end of my stick and as I flicked my wrist an eighth time the ground squirrel snagged on it and arched high above my head. I glanced quickly around, unsure where it had gone, and was about to look up when, with a dull splat, it bounced off my hardhat and landed on the paving at my feet.

For a moment, in the pickup, Leroy could not speak. Finally, he said the only thing that could settle my stomach: "That one's worth ten points."

Fortunately we had many chances for comic relief. After all, among the characters we met on our rounds were aging hippies seeking the psilocybin mushrooms rumored to grow in the park and a man who, accompanied by a dog and a cart-pulling pony, was traveling across the United States while subsisting on road kills like the ones we tossed off the highway.

Down deep, though, we took our work seriously, always looking for ways to make it easier. At Timber Lake trailhead, which doubled as a large picnic ground, we expected each morning to find the contents of eight fifty-gallon trash barrels scattered by hungry elk. At our urging, the park built a wooden corral around the barrels, but the elk pushed it down within days. Two large wooden boxes with heavy plywood lids came next. With the barrels placed inside, they succeeded in keeping the elk away but had the same effect on picnickers, who took to leaving dirty paper plates and chili cans in tidy piles under the tables. The foreman squelched our suggestion that the park buy the type of barrels used in Yellowstone to keep out bears, with locking lids and doors like mailbox slots. So we made do with the standard lids, dome-shaped with hinged doors, picking them up each day along with the trash and wiring them back on the barrels.

We were more successful in our lesser efforts at keeping the park clean. One day, seeing a man flick a lighted cigarette out of his car, Leroy slammed on our brakes, retrieved the cigarette, and chased him down. Pulling the man over, Leroy went to his window, handed him the smoldering butt and said, "This belongs to you."

It was then, I suppose, that we began looking at ourselves not as simple trash collectors but as conservation officers. We picked up where the rangers left off in their frustrating efforts to educate an environmentally unconscious public—but while the rangers only talked ecology, we actually got our hands dirty.

An incident one afternoon at a small picnic ground, just below timberline, strengthened us in our conviction. To enter the parking lot, Leroy had to guide the pickup around a widening stream of gray sludge that flowed toward the road from the open holding tank of a motor home.

"Would you look at that mess?" Leroy said.

He leaned heavily on the steering wheel. Until then, we had seen nothing to compare with this open cesspool. While any form of litter was baffling, this offense struck us both as beyond understanding since a waste water pumping station, where the RV's owner could have emptied the tank free of charge, lay only ten miles down the road.

We left the truck, gasping at the stench. By leaping a tendril of sewage, Leroy beat me to the motor home's Plexiglas door. Maybe the occupants read the righteous indignation on our faces. In any case, though we saw movement within and heard whispers, no one answered Leroy's knock. I stood at his shoulder and was about to attack the door with both fists when a green patrol car drove up and a park ranger got out.

This fifty-year-old seasonal employee, who spent his winters teaching high school biology, listened to our report with an aloof expression and dutifully bent to examine the open holding tank valve.

"You boys throw some dirt on this mess," he said.

We worked blindly, eyes on the ranger, our initial resentment at his command fading when he coaxed a white-haired man in a blue jumpsuit from the RV. The man demanded to know why the ranger had interrupted his lunch, and then went on to blame the spill on a young couple who had driven away in a camper just as he and his wife arrived. He was a good liar, sticking to his story even when confronted with the material evidence that soaked the parking lot.

After hearing him out, the ranger came over to say it was the old man's word against ours and the case probably wouldn't hold up if brought before the U.S. magistrate in Estes Park. The best he could do was issue a stern warning.

As the RV owner drove away, he met our stares with the upward thrust of a middle finger. The ranger clapped our shoulders and said, "I'm sure you boys understand." He pulled out of the parking area and left us to clean up the mess. Though still angry, we took from the incident a perverse satisfaction. We now had more ammunition in the on-going debate about which department—ranger or maintenance—was most vital to the operations of the park.

The debate, which cropped up at employee taco parties and could take a physical turn during west unit volleyball games, centered on the rangers' resentment of our higher pay and ours of their authority and holier-than-thou attitudes. As professional do-gooders, they sometimes had to risk their lives and often asked what we maintenance workers did to compare with that. In reply, the pump truck operator once remarked, "Any of you assholes ever stuck your arm up the honey wagon's hose to get a pop can some turkey threw in a pit toilet?"

Leroy and I, hard as we tried, never had the chance to match such selflessness. So it was with envy that I read several years later about a trash collector for the park's east unit who, seeing that a small reservoir's dam was about to burst, rushed down the mountain to warn the nearby town of Estes Park. His quick reaction allowed authorities to evacuate low-lying areas before the flood hit, perhaps saving lives. Despite my jealousy, reading about him made me truly proud for the first time to have been a park garbage man.

Leroy went on to a successful career with the State Department and seems to have managed to put his trash collector days behind him. I've tried to move on as well, but wherever I go the passing whiff of a back alley dumpster actually smells pretty good until I realize what it is.

An old Park Service buddy called recently to say that some of our exploits, like the Road Kill Olympics, had become part of park lore. This news pleased me until he added, "Even so, you'll never be as big as Captain Filth."

Waiting for Paramount

I was going to be famous.

Columbia, Disney, and Paramount Pictures were reading my unpublished first novel. My mentor, call him Barry, had traveled to Hollywood to make the pitch himself, lending the project his good name as the author of the screenplay. Barry also recommended I contact his editor at Random House, who agreed to read my manuscript when I put the final touches on it. An editor at *Outside*, also Barry's friend, read the first three chapters of the novel and hired me to write a personal essay about my experiences as a National Park trash collector (the topic of the book). At twenty-seven, I was a success—almost—and for that I could thank Barry.

I met him in 1982 at a summer writing workshop he held at his house, on a small ranch near Dallas. A professor at a Big Ten university, he had published three books, including a best-seller that helped pay for the ranch, on a wooded plateau topped by radio towers that jutted into the sky above the Texas landscape. He had also published essays in *Esquire*, *Harper's*, and *The New Yorker*. My wife—call her Rita—saw the ad for his workshop in a local arts magazine and urged me to sign up. A week before the workshop began I quit my job as a reporter for a business magazine to write fiction full time. My short-term goal: to write one chapter a week for eight weeks. My longer-term goal: to finish a first draft of the novel before our savings ran out.

The workshop met every Thursday night for three hours. A dozen writers from as far away as Waco paid $300 for the experience. I put the money down only after doing a careful investigation of Barry's background. Besides asking his university colleagues about him, I interviewed him and his wife, asking among other questions, "In your view, what are the chances of someone publishing a first novel?"

This question was crucial. That winter I had quit a fiction workshop at a Dallas community college when the instructor said, "A lot of fine work never gets published. For most writers, publishing is a pipe dream." To me, the remark sounded like loser-speak, the instructor's words made bitter by personal failure. Even if he spoke the truth, and perhaps he did, I could not afford to agree with him.

By contrast, Barry's answer rang with the authority of success: "The chances are excellent if the novel has an unusual concept and is well written." In fact, as a graduate student, Barry sold his first novel to W.W. Norton. His wife—call her Nadine—had published a nonfiction book about Texas women that sold more copies every year it was in print.

Satisfied, I handed over my check.

For the entire first week of self-employment, I shunned all distractions and knocked out a draft of chapter one. As I drove the winding road to Barry's ranch for the first session, I had a strong sense of embarking on an adventure, a sense clouded by the possibility that Barry and my classmates might not like my budding novel.

A dirt driveway led to an Austin-stone ranch house, complete with rocking chairs on the veranda and quilts on the walls. When I knocked, Nadine pointed me to a pathway that led around the main house to a log outbuilding. Inside were a long table, chairs for a dozen students, and a coffee pot. My fellow students were already at the table, pens, coffee cups, and manuscripts in front of them. A few chatted quietly, but most looked as intense as I felt. Three-fourths were women, ranging from recent college grads to middle-aged professionals. The only other male students were Charles, a retired accountant, and Wyatt, from Waco, who managed his family's cotton warehouses. We nodded and shook hands.

All talk ended when Barry entered the outbuilding as if walking onto a stage, clad in designer jeans, boat shoes, and a white peasant blouse, its top three buttons unfastened. He wore his graying hair combed back and slightly tousled. His lean build, Fu Manchu moustache, and narrow eyes gave him a rangy appearance. As I later learned, he came from a poor neighborhood in Dallas and took pride in having escaped his humble roots through the strategic use of intelligence and creativity.

That first night, we went around the table and described our projects. Most of my fellow students were memoirists or short story writers. Charles was writing a book of essays about his childhood to leave to his grandkids. Wyatt from Waco cited the works of Flannery O'Connor as most similar to his own. Sylvia, bejeweled, attractive, and silver blonde, was writing a collection of stories about the debutante set in Dallas. The only other aspiring novelist was Amber. Close to my age, with short dark hair and large brown eyes, Amber had a wide mouth that seldom smiled. A public relations rep, she regarded the rest of us with a cool reserve. She described her project as "a Southern Gothic exploration of life on the family ranch, which I intend to serve as a tribute to William Faulkner, my stylistic progenitor."

The idea sounded pretty good to me, but as she finished speaking, Barry frowned and let out a slow sigh—clearly not the feedback Amber anticipated. As our other classmates spoke, she went on staring at Barry, alarm frozen on her face.

Barry's reaction to Amber left me doubting my own idea. When it was my turn to speak, I gripped the edge of the table to keep my hands from shaking. "I just quit my job to write full time, so I'm a little freaked out," I said. "I'm working on a novel about a maintenance man who picks up trash in Rocky Mountain National Park. I hauled trash there for three summers, so I know the job, the setting, and the characters. And some crazy things happened, so I'm shooting for a sort of humorous detective story."

Barry smiled and shook his head. "It's like I told you before: publishing depends on finding an unusual concept and writing it well. You've got the concept. Now, do it justice."

Such praise did not sit well with Wyatt, Amber, and my other classmates, who perhaps hoped Barry would single them out, smile in wonder at their concept, anoint them as his literary heir apparent.

Thursday nights gave me weekly deadlines, and they sometimes came too soon. In groping for meaning, structure, and character in the raw first drafts of my chapters, I was turning out some bad prose—which Amber and Wyatt made clear. Each pointed to clichés and dangling modifiers as if issuing indictments. Guilty as charged, I could only nod and stare at the table. Even when I disagreed with a classmate's opinion, I could not speak. Barry's cardinal rule was that authors read their works aloud, submit to criticism, and thank their colleagues for the help. In spite of my classmates' negative reactions, Barry continued to see past my sentence-level blunders to the story taking shape and encouraged me to keep going.

He ran the workshop with a sure hand, using sarcasm and penetrating insight to maintain authority. "That's a fine sentence," he once told Amber, who almost smiled until he added, "Write ten thousand more like it, and you'll have a novel." He spoke with a cool understatement that made us fear and admire him. I noticed right away how some of the women responded, their faces flushing when he looked their way, their upper bodies turning to follow his movements around the room like flowers tracking the sun. Once, as we drank wine in a Dallas bar, he said, "Power is an aphrodisiac and in my workshops, I have the power."

In special weekend sessions, he read aloud the worst passages of my novel in his slow Texas drawl. I nearly suffocated, my laughter hurting the soul as much as the belly. As a mentor, Barry understood my half-expressed thoughts. He had the gift of intuiting my intentions for a character or storyline and giving advice that took me there. I often felt as if his brain encompassed mine—as if he knew all my thoughts and ideas, but on a higher and more artistic level. This sensation is hard to describe, and I later realized it was illusory. I knew a lot of things Barry did not, but he was good at making me like and need him. And he *was* helping me.

At the end of eight weeks, I met my first goal. Barry suggested I stop there and spend the next two months revising the first eight chapters, which I would ship to him for feedback at the end of September. If they looked okay, I would pick up the story from chapter nine and try to finish a draft before his summer workshop reconvened.

Rita and I had already decided to return to the Rockies, where we met. She would find a job, and I would work on the book. A registered nurse, she could get a job anywhere by walking into a local hospital, so we packed our car with camping gear and my typewriter and went west to find a place to live. After a two-month loop through Utah, Idaho, Montana, and Wyoming, we settled in Durango, Colorado. All winter, as Rita worked the evening shift at Durango's Mercy Medical Center, I sat in our cold, shabby duplex, next door to the city's leading drug dealer, and cranked out chapters. Though still supportive, Rita asked me often when I thought I might finish. Her friends at work expressed open incredulity at the notion of a stay-at-home novelist husband, and one implied I was taking unfair advantage of her. In response, I accepted some free-lance reporting jobs, which brought in a few thousand but also slowed my progress on the novel. Most days, I sat shivering at the typewriter, trying to focus while my neighbor sold cocaine to college kids and screamed at his girlfriend.

In the spring, with all but the final two chapters drafted, I learned Barry was having hard times of his own. Our workshop would meet at an arts center in Dallas, instead of his ranch, because his marriage was over. As Barry told me, he had asked Nadine for a divorce because "the spark is gone."

When I arrived in Texas for the workshop, Barry asked for my help moving file cabinets and other belongings out of the ranch house, part of his settlement with Nadine. He went through a stack of love letters and said he hadn't realized how badly he'd hurt her until he saw her the night before. Suddenly fragile, he said, "I'm thinking of calling off the divorce—for now." Though inexperienced in such matters, I said, "Don't you do it, Barry, unless you mean to stay in the marriage. You'll only hurt her more." He pondered my advice and agreed. We left the house as friends, or so I thought at the time.

My parents lived in Dallas, so I stayed with them during the workshop, making the drive home to Durango twice a month to spend time with Rita. She was happier now because Barry had spoken to the William Morris Agency about basing a screenplay on my novel, and halfway through the workshop he flew to Hollywood to pitch the concept. The only studio to bite—Paramount—was already talking money: $75,000 for me, as creative consultant, and twice that for Barry, as writer of the screenplay.

"Why can't we collaborate on the screenplay?" I asked. "I could use the experience—and the money. After all, it's my novel."

Barry's eyes narrowed. "That's why you're the creative consultant. Someday, maybe you can get better terms through your own agent."

His tone mixed regret with an implied threat, and I dropped the issue. Our big payday hinged on the approval of Paramount's top producer, but meanwhile Barry announced our news to the workshop, whose members acted suitably impressed and envious. Amber turned a sharp gaze on me. "You're lucky you could quit your job. If the rest of us could do that, maybe *we* could get a movie deal."

Barry fixed her with a cool stare. "It's not about luck. He's taking a high-stakes gamble that's about to pay off."

At that moment, I felt a profound affection for Barry, who understood my situation better even than Rita or my parents. If I suspected him sometimes of taking unfair advantage, he also inspired in me a strong personal loyalty.

Soon, though, whenever I tried to exert my own growing sense of authority, Barry issued harsh criticisms and reminders of how much I owed him. As he said, "I'm giving you in a few months what I spent a quarter century learning. The least you can do is to show me some gratitude." My gratitude took the form of après-workshop drinks, bottles of champagne with which to toast our successes, and my company on weekend trips to strip clubs. I often wondered if our visits to the establishments on Greenville Avenue in Dallas were Barry's attempts to drive a wedge between Rita and me, but I never asked about his motives. In exchange for his help and access to his agent and editors, I did what he asked. In one such joint, having had several drinks, he said, "From now on, for you everything's *gratis*. You can take my workshops anytime you like, free of charge."

We touched glasses, and I said, "Here's to a long—and rich—collaboration."

Such warmth faded by early July when I missed a party Sylvia threw at her Dallas home in Barry's honor. I spent that evening trying to put a decent ending on the novel. Paramount's top producer was waiting for my last chapter, Barry said, which would sell or kill the screenplay. The deadline drove everything else, including Sylvia's party, from my mind.

Angry as a jilted lover, Barry said he forgave me after he read the ending, but for a while Sylvia became the anointed one. My lesser status in the workshop did not liberate me. Instead, Barry only made greater demands. During one of our strip joint forays, he looked across the table, and his eyes grew hard above his wine glass. "After what I've done for you, we'd be sleeping together by now if you were a woman."

I laughed uneasily. "Sorry, but you're not my type."

"You have sisters, don't you?"

"Three. You're not their type either, Barry."

Then he arrived at the real point. "There's Rita."

No longer amused, I stared across the table at him. "What about her?"

"She should be feeling grateful enough about now."

I walked out of the bar and nearly drove home to Colorado. *Coward*, I berated myself. *You should have knocked the smirk off the bastard's face.* For a few days, I refused to take Barry's calls. I soon realized, though, that even if he had crossed the line, crossed several lines, we had a stake in each other. Our partnership gave him power over me, but it also gave me some power to resist when he acted too much like himself.

Cool now to each other, we sat in his apartment one Friday night with his support system of well-known Texas writers and waited for the call from Paramount. If the phone rang by seven o'clock Texas time, we had a deal. In anticipation, we opened the champagne and joked about all the luxuries we would buy with our windfall. In my case, Rita was shopping for a washer and dryer. She had also spoken to a realtor about purchasing a house on a hill overlooking Durango. We could almost afford it if the advance came through. By nine o'clock, still waiting for a call that didn't come, we drank the rest of the champagne to take the edge off our despair.

Rita took the news hard.

I reminded her that Random House would soon read my novel and *Outside*'s editors liked the early drafts of my essay, but by sharing my dream with her, I had raised her hopes, and now nothing but a movie deal would do.

On my last night in Dallas, Barry told me to keep working. "If you like, I'll have a talk with Rita—keep her off your back."

I put up both hands: "No thanks."

Shortly after Barry's second summer workshop, my chances for fame fell through. Random House passed on the novel, *Outside* killed the essay, and Rita insisted I go back into journalism. Instead, I entered an MFA program and spent the next two years polishing my writing skills and learning to teach. To Rita's credit, though the spark was gone, she tolerated my tarnished dream long enough to get me through school and into a teaching job. To Barry's credit, he steered me to a New York agent once I finished a sixth draft of the novel.

I saw Barry for the last time in a hotel bar, five years after our first workshop. We met to reminisce and to transfer into his hands my gift of his favorite champagne. The plan: to call him when the agent agreed to take me on and celebrate this event by popping the corks of identical bottles of Brut. Barry arrived an hour late, with a well-dressed but drunken woman whose gait drew my gaze to her prosthetic leg. He introduced her as "Margot." For twenty minutes, Barry and I tried to talk while Margot interrupted with loud and suggestive remarks about their plans. "Let's go, I'm bored," she said and tugged his arm. He finally let her drag him to the parking lot. She got behind the wheel of a small sports car and revved the engine while he and I shook hands.

"Be sure to save the champagne for our toast," I said as he got into the car. He promised he would. Margot laid rubber as they sped away.

Three months later, I phoned Barry. "It's good news! Get out the champagne."

He laughed. "Remember Margot, the one-legged woman? We drank your bottle that night in her hotel room."

Before she left me, Rita suggested Barry had jinxed my novel—and our marriage—by opening the champagne early. I believe other forces were at work. My agent tried for two years but could not sell the book. With three decades of hindsight, I can see I was not yet writer enough to

43

withstand Barry's help. He taught me a lot in a short time: intentional lessons about writing, yes, but also unintentional lessons about avoiding dependency, abuses of power, and the crossing of lines. I still put these lessons to use in mentoring young writers. As for Barry, he gave me opportunities most writers get only after decades of hard, solitary work, and it was up to me to rise to the challenge, which I did not do. Twenty years after my first workshop session at Barry's ranch, I wrote, and published, a second novel.

I'm still waiting to hear from Paramount Pictures.

The Psychology of Littering

I brought our pickup to an abrupt stop, causing trash to shift forward in the bed. Fifty feet back, in the grass along the road, something unnatural had caught my partner Leroy's eye. He ran back for it and reappeared a moment later with a disposable diaper pinched between two fingers.

In a mournful voice, Leroy said, "How could anyone drive through the most beautiful place in the world, roll down the window, and toss out a Pampers?"

We asked this question often during three summers spent picking up litter in Rocky Mountain National Park, but we never came up with an acceptable answer. Fifteen years later, still seeking one, I've turned to naturalists, psychologists, and sociologists for help. But few address the question directly. Like Henry David Thoreau, they often speak of the rejuvenating powers of wilderness but seem to overlook the price of renewal. For in loving nature, and drawing strength from it, we take more than pictures and leave more than footprints. Indeed, we leave behind the worst parts of ourselves. The easiest answer as to why people defile their most beloved park lands is that litterers are vandals with little sense of the damage they do, whose parents raised them badly. This explanation may be true in part, but litterers do more than show a casual disregard for the environment. For many, littering may provide a means of asserting personal freedom, setting territory, even soothing fears; people may mark the wilderness to make it less threatening. Littering may also be a necessary catharsis—the material expression of psychic garbage. If so, then for litterers, and perhaps for all of us, the wilderness may serve as both spiritual recharger and psychic trash dump.

Naturalist Ann Zwinger illustrates the damage littering does to fragile tundra, where trash takes decades to biodegrade. Even the smallest piece of litter, she says, "cuts the light to the plants it covers, killing them within a few weeks" and "Fifty to one hundred years of plant growth can be snuffed out by a beer can" (381). The Park Service posts anti-littering signs, issues tickets up to $500, and prints pamphlets to educate park visitors about the damage being done. Yet despite the agency's best efforts, tourists go right on littering.

Social psychologists call littering and vandalism *depreciative behavior*. At first glance, then, we may assume that people who litter find little to appreciate in the wilderness. The time and money they spend getting there, however, contradicts this assumption. While working Trail Ridge Road, I overheard many tourists reverently remark on the gorgeous vistas. All too often, after they took a photograph, the same people wadded up a film box or a candy wrapper and casually threw it off the viewpoint.

Such conflicting behavior is in no way simple and, as I've suggested, goes beyond ignorance and apathy. To understand it, we might begin by asking why litterers bother to visit national parks. What are they seeking? Complex though the answer may be, chances are they're looking for some of the same things as the rest of us—beauty, solitude, fresh air, a sense of renewal. As Thoreau says, "When I would recreate myself, I seek the darkest wood" (183), from which "come the tonics and barks which brace mankind" (181). John Burroughs, too, went to the wilds "to be soothed and healed, to have my senses put in tune once more" (274).

But perhaps our depreciative tourists are seeking something more tangible than were Thoreau and Burroughs. Perhaps they're after a token of what's rare and good in nature—a fistful of wild flowers, a chunk of petrified wood, a snapshot of breathtaking scenery—one last memento of the vanishing abundance. Nature writer John Fowles notes that "man is a highly acquisitive creature" with "a constant need to seek new objects" (660). This need may express itself in the fever of thrill seeking and peak bagging, which in recent decades has rekindled in the most round-bellied of flatlanders, some of whom are daring even to collect fourteeners. As our wilderness dwindles, even our most environmentally attuned hope to grab what they can, as the following passage from Edward Abbey's *Desert Solitaire* suggests:

> Standing there, gaping at this monstrous and inhuman spectacle of rock and cloud and sky and space, I feel a ridiculous greed... come over me. I want to know it all, possess it all, embrace the entire scene intimately, deeply, totally, as a man desires a beautiful woman. (5)

Most of us, then, including litterers, want to sample the beauty and bounty of the wilderness. If these qualities fail to move us, however, there's always the promise of freedom. Who among us hasn't dreamed of wandering wherever our legs would carry us, answering to no authority but our own? Abbey tasted such freedom and urged the Park Service to grant tourists the same privilege, saying, "for Godsake, let them get lost, sunburnt, stranded, drowned, eaten by bears, buried alive under avalanches—that is the right of any free American" (*Desert Solitaire* 55-56). In the wilderness a person can escape the restrictions of "excessive industrialism," he writes. Our wildlands might also someday provide "a refuge from ...political oppression," a base "for guerrilla warfare against tyranny" (130).

But while wilderness serves as a symbol of freedom, tourists confront a different reality. Laws aimed at protecting our parks and wilderness areas seem to restrict their every move: Don't collect firewood, flowers, or berries, they're told. Don't fish, hunt, or camp without a permit. Above all, don't litter.

These well-meaning restrictions may actually drive some tourists to commit acts of depreciation. Psychologist Daniel Stokols writes that when crowding (and presumably restrictive laws) threaten personal freedom, an individual may attempt to reestablish it "through the enactment of ... forbidden or threatened behavior" (257). That this behavior might include littering Abbey illustrates through the following scene in *The Monkey Wrench Gang*. Seldom Seen Smith says,

> "Any road I wasn't consulted about that I don't like, I litter. It's my religion."
> "Right," Hayduke said. "Litter the shit out of them."
> "Well now," the doctor said. "I hadn't thought about that. Stockpile the stuff along the highways. Throw it out the window. Well... why not?"
> "Doc," said Hayduke, "it's liberation." (65)

Abbey hits his target, as usual, and in the process captures a part of the psychology of littering—the quiet exultation that comes from defying authority. Like Seldom Seen, many Americans may resent the government's failure to consult them before building roads like Trail Ridge. Recalling the number of diapers I picked up in my brief career, thousands of Americans certainly are littering the shit out of their highways. Of course, having been on the receiving end of these acts of rebellion, I find unacceptable the morality that equates tossing a beer can with casting a ballot for emancipation. Besides, research by forester Richard C. Knopf counters the image of litterer as lonely freedom fighter. Knopf divides tourists into "escape-oriented veterans" and "the relative newcomer" most interested in group activities like picnicking (210). He found the car-bound picnickers to be significantly "more opposed to management regulations intended to control their personal behavior than the ... Type 1 veterans" (210). So it follows that Knopf's Type 2—similar to the "mechanized tourist" Abbey berates in *Desert Solitaire* (49)—is more prone than, say, an Earth First! member to litter our wilderness in the name of liberty.

Those unmoved by the need to assert their freedom may litter to express the ancient, and related, need to establish territory. I say related because by setting territorial boundaries people define a secured space within which they're free to work, live, or play. As Sociologist William R. Catton, Jr. writes:

> Every species "uses"the environments upon which it depends in three basic ways: (1) as a place in which to carry on its activities, (2) as a source of supplies required for those activities, and (3) as a repository for the material products of those activities (e.g., effluents). (283)

Legally, our species may use the national parks mainly in the first way: as a place for activities. In theory, we must pack in our supplies and pack out our refuse—or deposit it in the proper receptacle. That many of the 300 million citizens with whom we share ownership of these lands fail to do so can, perhaps, be seen as a regression to more natural land-use habits. But it may also be their way of marking a temporary territory. Environmental psychologists Irwin Altman and Martin M. Chemers point out that animals use "excretions, secretions, noise and other means, as signals to potential intruders and perhaps as reminders to themselves where their places begin and end" (138). People, they add, usually mark territories with "artifacts and symbols; they rarely use secretions or excretions" (138). I assert that people use secretions to mark territory more often than Altman and Chemers suspect, but let's begin with their use of artifacts. In national parks, the most common temporary territories are fishing holes and campsites. Leroy and I believed we could tell the best fishing holes along a given lake or stream by the number of discarded beer cans we found. Changing brand names even told us where one hole ended and another began, as if the space an angler needed matched the distance he or she could cast an empty can. As for campsites, the presence of a tent, cooler, or other artifact usually establishes a claim. An off-duty ranger tells of having left a water jug to hold a campsite in Glacier National Park. He went fishing and returned hours later to find his site occupied. The claim jumpers denied they'd ever seen his jug. "We've been here for hours," one said, and as proof pointed to the litter strewn about the site. Later, the ranger found his missing jug in a nearby trash barrel.

On a backcountry ski trip, the same ranger and I set the effective limits of a campsite through our choice of where to urinate in the snow. Perhaps this was not a conscious act of territoriality, but when other skiers threatened to camp too close, our suggestion as to where they should pitch their tents lay outside the area we'd marked—and meant to defend.

Like gangs marking their turf with spray paint, a more technologically advanced secretion, tourists use graffiti as a lasting statement of ownership. Notice the names, dates, four-letter words, and declarations of love carved into aspens or painted on boulders near heavy-use areas. Like littering, these brands leave few doubts that tourists have had an impact on a place—changed it and, in a small way, made it theirs.

In so altering the immediate environment, they may seek not simply to keep others out, but to make the wilderness—perhaps nature itself—seem smaller, more manageable, and less frightening. Stokols writes that when "an individual's supply of space greatly exceeds his demand," he will tend to "experience a need for enclosure and affiliation with others" (248). This need may explain why some park visitors never leave their cars. Those who do may combat fear of what they see as a threatening wasteland with a depreciative act, such as throwing a beer can.

This action has several immediate effects: First, it makes nature seem more familiar, and therefore safer. Second, it degrades the wilderness, literally making it smaller. Third, it allows a person to express contempt for an otherwise awe-inspiring natural feature—like a teenager who says of the Grand Canyon, "Big deal, the world's biggest pit."

At Rocky Mountain National Park, tourists often timidly asked, "Do people ever miss a curve and drive over a cliff?" or "How often are hikers mauled by bears?" to which we were tempted to reply, "Not often enough." But as absurd as the questions seemed, they revealed genuine fears deeply rooted in our culture. Altman and Chemers note that "uncontrolled nature and the wilderness were historically viewed in Western society as dangerous..." (19). Although purged of the grizzly and the marauding Indian, and reduced to a point where we need to protect it from ourselves, the tame remnant of our wilderness continues to color our imaginations, inspiring some but terrifying others.

These feelings are often based entirely on fantasy. In fact, as Leroy and I saw it, our main purpose in collecting trash was to maintain the illusion that Rocky Mountain National Park was a pristine wilderness. Two of our supervisors made this task more difficult by regularly knocking buckets of golf balls into Forest Canyon (and bragging to all who would listen that they could hit a two wood farther than Arnold Palmer). Yet we never doubted the importance of our work, and it turns out we were right since people's feelings, based on fantasy or reality, influence not only how they perceive the wilderness but how they treat it. According to Knopf, "People transform reality by imposing their own order on incoming stimuli..." (223). As a result, "The environments people see are, in part, created by the mind" (223) and "images held by recreationists affect their behavior" (225), including littering and vandalism.

Veteran hikers may see a national park as benign, even in need of protection, while novices see it as a place full of hidden danger, a place they must control (or alter) to feel safe. This need, often expressed as an attempt to reduce or conquer, is "incompatible with much of what wilderness offers and demands," say Kaplan and Talbot (194). They tell of urban teens in an Outdoor Challenge program, who by gaining wilderness experience learned that insisting on control is a "costly and disturbing preoccupation" (194).

Like these enlightened teens, people with a close connection to nature may feel less need for control and, consequently, be less apt to commit acts of depreciation. Joseph Wood Krutch supports this idea in describing his urge to destroy a beautiful ice crystal:

> I resisted, I am proud to say, the almost universal impulse to scratch my initials into one of the surfaces.... The impulse to mar and to destroy is as ancient and almost as nearly universal ... as the impulse to create. The one is an easier way than the other of demonstrating power. (443)

Unfortunately, even those who overcome their destructive impulses litter the wilderness with human waste, solid and psychic. As I've said, in deriving benefits from the wilderness, we leave behind the worst parts of ourselves—our trash, sewage, sweat, stress, and anxiety. We practice this catharsis either directly, meaning to purge ourselves of such poisons, or indirectly, as a by-product of recreation.

Consider the tossing of a Pampers. The parents of an infant, finding the atmosphere of their car suddenly toxic, take direct action to purify it, refusing even to wait until they reach a trash barrel. One day, at a scenic overlook, Leroy and I came across a more extreme example of direct catharsis. A widening stream of sewage flowed onto the tundra from the bowels of a motor home. The creators of this open cesspool sat inside the RV, enjoying the view and a picnic lunch. This act seemed especially baffling since each of the park's campgrounds had a waste water dumping station. Stranger still was the owners' lack of remorse, as if dumping sewage were an acceptable practice in the national parks.

If we view their act of depreciation dispassionately, we can almost understand their attitude. Burroughs writes of one day finding several birds and insects drowned in a bucket of maple sap. He emptied this "bucketful of corruption" onto the ground, knowing it would "soon be made sweet and wholesome again by the chemistry of the soil" (275). For early Christians the wilderness "served a purification... function," with leaders going to the desert to cleanse their souls (Altman and Chemers 19). Even today, we value the "psychological products" of outdoor activities more than the activities themselves, Knopf says, citing studies that show sixty percent of Americans visit "natural environments largely to alleviate stress" (207). Like nature writer J.A. Baker, perhaps the polluters of our scenic viewpoint only "longed to be a part of the outward life, to... let the human taint wash away in emptiness and silence as the fox sloughs his smell into the cold unworldliness of water..." (653).

While our wilderness was vast, we could happily go about washing away the taint. Now, such high-use areas as river beaches where rafters camp accumulate "charcoal, human waste, and other debris...faster than the river can purge them" (Catton 289). And as the wilderness shrinks, so does its capacity to purify even our psychic trash. The "truest devotees can overuse an environment," Catton says, and "even the nonconsumptive forms of recreation conforming to the motto 'Take only pictures, leave only footprints' can be engaged in excessively" (284). On top of other damage, a simple hike to relieve tensions can "turn trails into ruts and greatly accelerate soil erosion" (Chase 210).

So where does this leave us? In answer to Leroy's question, people will litter the world's most beautiful places to assert personal freedom, mark territory, control their fears, and purge themselves of toxins. The logical next question is this: If even our most benign, low-impact users irreparably harm the wilderness, can we do anything—beyond toilet training tourists—to slow the degradation of our wildlands?

With so many forces arrayed on the side of littering, a person can't help feeling pessimistic. The only sure solution may be to close the backcountry or to so restrict access that nature can repair any damages. This drastic measure would conflict, however, with government policies aimed at making wildlands more accessible. Worse, in further distancing us from nature, it might also revive our age-old desire to make the wasteland safe. So in exchange for the "incomparable sanity [wilderness] can bring briefly... into our insane lives" (Stegner 565), perhaps we must accept the inadvertent damage that nature lovers do and put our energy into preventing intentional acts of depreciation.

Tougher littering laws may only inspire rebellion. Likewise, government efforts to force responsibility on tourists by refusing to pick up their trash often fail. Certainly, as Zwinger observes, "The mother who always picks up after her children soon finds that is all she does" (381), but too many tourists lack responsibility. And as Knopf points out, people "read the recreation site itself" to determine "what forms of behavior are appropriate" (221). Thus, if tourists see litter on the ground, they're more likely to add to the clutter.

Futile though it seems, perhaps our best hope lies in continuing to pick up their litter and in helping them to understand, as John Steinbeck did, that by going to the wilderness "we become forever a part of it; that our rubber boots slogging through a flat of eelgrass...make us truly and permanently a factor in the ecology"; that "We shall take something away from it, but we shall leave something too" (503).

Works Cited

Abbey, Edward. *Desert Solitaire*. New York: McGraw-Hill, 1968. Print.

---. *The Monkey Wrench Gang*. 1975. New York: Avon, 1976. Print.

Altman, Irwin and Martin Chemers. *Culture and Environment*. Monterey: Brooks/Cole, 1980. Print.

Baker, J.A. "From The Peregrine." 1967. *The Norton Book of Nature Writing*. Ed. Robert Finch and John Elder. New York: Norton, 1990. 652-57. Print.

Burroughs, John. "The Gospel of Nature." 1912. *The Norton Book of Nature Writing*. Eds. Robert Finch and John Elder. New York: Norton, 1990. 273-79. Print.

Catton, William R., Jr. "Social and Behavioral Aspects of Carrying Capacity of Natural Environments." 1983. *Behavior and the Natural Environment*. Eds. Irwin Altman and Joachim F. Wohlwill. New York: Premium, 1987. 269-306. Print.

Chase, Alston. *Playing God in Yellowstone*. New York: Harvest/HBJ, 1987. Print.

Fowles, John. "From *The Tree*." 1979. *The Norton Book of Nature Writing*. Eds. Robert Finch and John Elder. New York: Norton, 1990. 657-70. Print.

Kaplan, Stephen and Janet Frey Talbot. "Psychological Benefits of a Wilderness Experience." 1983. *Behavior and the Natural Environment*. Eds. Irwin Altman and Joachim F. Wohlwill. New York: Premium, 1987. 163-204. Print.

Knopf, Richard C. "Recreational Needs and Behavior in Natural Settings." 1983. *Behavior and the Natural Environment*. Eds. Irwin Altman and Joachim F. Wohlwill. New York: Premium, 1987. 205-40. Print.

Krutch, Joseph Wood. "The Colloid and the Crystal." 1953. *The Norton Book of Nature Writing*. Eds. Robert Finch and John Elder. New York: Norton, 1990. 442-49. Print.

Sherwood, Steve. "In the Footsteps of Captain Filth." *Northern Lights*. Jan.-Feb. 1986: 4-5. Print.

Stegner, Wallace. "Coda: Wilderness Letter." 1960. *The Norton Book of Nature Writing*. Eds. Robert Finch and John Elder. New York: Norton, 1990. 564-69. Print.

Steinbeck, John. "From *The Log from the Sea of Cortez*. 1951.*The Norton Book of Nature Writing*. Eds. Robert Finch and John Elder. New York: Norton, 1990. 501-4. Print.

Stokols, Daniel. "A Social-Psychological Model of Human Crowding Phenomena." 1972. *Human Behavior and the Environment: Interactions Between Man and His Physical World*. Ed. John H. Sims and Duane D. Baumann. Chicago: Maaroufa, 1974. 240-62. Print.

Thoreau, Henry David. "Walking." 1863. *The Norton Book of Nature Writing*. Eds. Robert Finch and John Elder. New York: Norton, 1990. 181-88. Print.

Zwinger, Ann H. and Beatrice E. Willard. *Land Above the Trees: A Guide to American Alpine Tundra*. New York: Perennial Library, 1972. Print.

Environmentalist as Misanthrope

Twenty years ago, I ambushed David Brower on his way to dinner after he delivered the keynote address to an international wilderness conference. An issue had bothered me for a long time, and I felt sure Brower, my hero and the former president of the Sierra Club, the archdruid himself (McPhee), could resolve it. As he passed, I said, "Mr. Brower, may I ask you something?"

Brower stopped and stared, which I took to mean yes.

"Will the environmental movement ever grow beyond misanthropy?" I asked. "Will we someday reach a stage where we can love the earth *and* ourselves, or will our love of the land and our dismay at the harm we've done it only lead us deeper into self-hatred?"

Brower regarded me fiercely for a while. Then one of his retinue suggested they go in, and my chance passed. I like to think Brower was actually giving the idea some thought, that he found it too intriguing and complex to formulate a quick answer. Or maybe he was hungry. Unresolved, the issue has continued to fester. Edward Abbey sums up the misanthropic side of the environmental movement in *Desert Solitaire* when he says, "I'm a humanist. I'd rather kill a *man* than a snake" (17). Abbey may have made this statement in jest, but it expresses a feeling shared by many who love the earth, including me. Having grown up on the Colorado Front Range, I've experienced the fear and rage that accompany the loss of a cherished landscape. I've felt suffocated by crowding and sickened at the sight of buildings where wildlife once ran. My disillusionment deepened after I spent three summers picking up America's trash in Rocky Mountain National Park. Like most environmentalists, I identify so closely with certain special places that I feel physical pain on seeing them ruined. And I'll admit my agony has at times evolved into a full-blown misanthropy, a hatred not only of those directly responsible for the destruction, but of all the filthy, wasteful members of our species. This hatred troubles me because of its impact on my life and because of its potential impact on the movement if others share it. A love of nature is crucial in our fight to save the environment. Taken too far, though, our love may degrade into misanthropy; our hatred of humankind in general may further degrade into self-hatred; once we hate ourselves, we may lose the capacity for the love of nature that, having twisted into hate, began this process; and this loss may rob the movement of those who, loving the earth, would seek to protect it.

First, a disclaimer: I'm not some anti-environmentalist seeking a new way to bash the movement. Nor am I an apologist for Earth First!, who in the spirit of Abbey's *The Monkey Wrench Gang* has declared war on the military-industrial complex. I'll admit to a bias, though, because I view environmentalists as a force for good in the world. In striving to save what's left of Earth's wilderness, they pit themselves against the forces of waste and destruction. Brower himself has written that even the most fanatical of monkey wrenchers (the tree spikers and wreckers of bulldozers commonly referred to as eco-terrorists) are joyous lovers of life: "They laugh hard, work hard, and don't mind a beer or two" while they fight "for community, kinship, freedom, beauty, love, and justice for all—humans, other animals, land, air, water, plants" (Scarce xi). In this way, at least, environmentalists fit Erich Fromm's portrait of the biophilous person. *Biophilia*, he says, "is the passionate love of life and of all that is alive; it is the wish to further growth, whether in a person, a plant, an idea, or a social group" (406). Like some environmentalists, the biophilous person defines *good* as "a reverence for life, all that enhances life, growth, unfolding" and *evil* as "all that stifles life, narrows it down, cuts it into pieces" (406). Examples of biophilous persons include Ghandi and Albert Schweitzer (408). Thoreau, Muir, and Leopold might also qualify, having committed themselves to saving the wild cradle of life.

But Abbey complicates any attempt to equate biophilia and environmentalism. Never one to blush at contradiction, this self-described misanthrope was a father of five (*Hayduke Lives!* preface). He mixed a loathing for humanity, except perhaps friends and family, with a love of the Colorado Plateau that approached the erotic. As he reflects in *Desert Solitaire*,

> Standing there, gaping at this monstrous and inhuman spectacle of rock and cloud and sky and space, I feel a ridiculous greed . . . come over me. I want to know it all, possess it all, embrace the entire scene intimately, deeply, totally, as a man desires a beautiful woman. (6)

In likening an inhuman landscape to a beautiful woman, this passage adds meaning to the term *nature lover*. It also reveals Abbey's paradoxical desires: (1) his longing to blend so utterly with the landscape that he and it become one; (2) his need to anthropomorphize the landscape to imagine how this joining might occur; and (3) an all-too-human yearning to claim the land he loves but cannot own. In plainer words, for a union to occur, Abbey must deny his humanity or the landscape must become human. Neither contingency can happen, so Abbey must form a far less satisfying link, based on what amounts to spiritual ownership of the land. He is not alone in loving and identifying with a landscape. Sociologists call this condition *topophilia* and say it often "'evokes pride of ownership'" (Brown and Perkins 281).

If I understand Abbey's topophilic yearnings, it's because I lust after the Colorado Rockies, especially the Rampart Range where I grew up. Legally the land I love belongs to others, or to all of us, but spiritually it remains mine. I claimed it as a child by walking across it, by touching it, and by learning the names of its trees and wild flowers. As an adolescent, I found freedom from peers and parents at the top of the sandstone cliff in my father's backyard. Ranging the pocket of wilderness beyond--still inhabited by mountain lions--shaped me, tied my sense of identity to a landscape of joy and life and freedom. Years later, my best experiences as a Park Service trash man continued this process. Rocky Mountain National Park, the heart of the Rockies, became for me "the ideal place, the right place, the one true home" (Abbey, *Desert Solitaire* 1). Like doing household chores, fetching the Pampers and Coors cans tourists scattered along Trail Ridge Road gave me proprietary feelings, a stake in the park's ecology. I cleansed the landscape of filth, returned it daily to what approximated a pristine state. In my mind, I became a part of the park and the park became a part of me.

Unfortunately, when we identify with a landscape we don't own, we lack the power to control its fate. And this lack becomes a problem when its legal owners cherish their property not for intangible qualities, such as beauty, but for tangible ones, such as the profits they can make by carving it up. I first encountered this conflict of values as a child, when a gravel company began mining a mountain near Colorado Springs. Perched northwest of Garden of the Gods—sacred to the Utes—the mine marred the westward view. My father explained all about mineral rights and free enterprise, but at age seven I found unfathomable that anyone might rip apart and haul away the top half of a mountain. Later, as a trash man, although grown used to seeing tourists litter my park, an event at a scenic viewpoint one day struck me as truly puzzling: A widening stream of sewage flowed onto the tundra from the bowels of a motor home, while the owners sat inside, eating lunch. The park's campgrounds had wastewater dumping stations, so this crime seemed especially pointless. Stranger still was the owners' lack of remorse, as if dumping sewage were standard practice in a national park.

Intuitively I saw this act—and the earlier decapitation of the mountain—as alien. Abbey echoes this notion after meeting a surveyor who insists Arches National Park needs a paved road to attract more tourists. "I knew I was dealing with a madman," he says (*Desert Solitaire* 51). The perception that ravagers of the landscape are alien or insane may sound ludicrous, but it plays a key role in turning topophiles into misanthropes. Fromm lends additional support to this notion, pointing to psychological differences between biophilous persons, drawn magnetically to light, growth, and life, and necrophilous persons, drawn to destruction and death. He defines *necrophilia* as "*the passion to transform that which is alive into something unalive; to destroy for the sake of destruction; the exclusive interest in all that is purely mechanical. It is the passion to tear apart living structures*" (369, emphasis in original).

I'm tempted to classify all litterbugs, land developers, and heads of such agencies as the Bureau of Land Management and the Army Corps of Engineers as necrophiles. Some no doubt deserve this label. But as Fromm points out, except Adolf Hitler and your average serial killer, few people qualify as purely necrophilous. Most of us fall between the poles, drawn at various times toward each. And just as we cannot peg Abbey as a biophile, we cannot peg all who harm the land as necrophiles. Still, Fromm blames many of society's ills, including pollution, on what he calls the "marketing personality." Like necrophiles, marketing persons turn their interest "away from life, persons, nature, ideas—in short from everything that is alive" (389) and focus on "mechanical, nonalive artifacts" (381). Such persons, Fromm implies, would love an iPad more than a spouse. Driven chiefly by profit, they view nature, land, even other people as commodities (388). The marketing person, "in the name of progress, is transforming the world into a stinking and poisonous place . . . . He pollutes the air, the water, the animals—and himself . . . to a degree that has made it doubtful whether the earth will still be livable within a hundred years from now" (389).

We topophiles find marketing persons hard to fathom but easy to hate. After all, the destruction of landscapes we love, whether motivated by greed or a necrophilous urge to tear apart a living structure, amounts to a personal attack. It robs us of the happiness and freedom wilderness provides. Abbey predicts Americans may one day need wilderness "not only as a refuge from excessive industrialism but also as a refuge from . . . political oppression" (*Desert Solitaire* 149). He indirectly links such oppression to Fromm's marketing personality, saying, "Technology adds a new dimension . . . by providing modern despots with instruments [of tyranny] far more efficient than any available to their classical counterparts" (149). So perhaps we can understand why, faced with a population that equates land development with progress, the outnumbered, outgunned topophile may come to see humankind as the enemy.

My own transformation came a decade after my sometimes-bitter experiences as a trash collector. Living in Durango, Colorado, I took daily walks up a small wooded valley near my home. The valley provided winter forage for elk, and I nearly always encountered wildlife. As before, I didn't own the land, but I loved it. Indeed, I felt so protective of it that during a hike I once insisted my mother put back a piece of weathered piñon she fancied. Taking so extreme a stand for preservation seemed absurd a year later when the landowners bulldozed the valley, scraping away nearly every bush and tree. The contractor who planned to build houses there subsequently went bankrupt, leaving the landscape barren and eroded.

I'm unsure why this particular event had such an impact. After all, I'd seen other special places ruined. And though I'd hated the individuals (like the RV driver) who did the actual damage, these episodes hadn't soured me on humankind. But anger that had brewed for years suddenly jelled. I felt hemmed in, fearful of a future without beauty, hopeless in the face of a locust-like civilization that chewed up and spit out the land. The joy the Rockies once gave me turned to bitterness, and rather than exult in the beauty that remained, I mourned the losses. The sight of roads, dams, or power lines—any fresh mark on the land—enraged me. I wanted my valley back, and my mountaintop, and Rocky Mountain National Park. And while the gods were at it, I also wanted the buffalo, the wolf, and the other species that vanished with the wild lands. In short, having found present-day nature in many ways flawed, I wanted a return to the way things were at some undefined point in the past, preferably before the white onslaught, and I didn't particularly care if my desires were idealistic or carried unpleasant implications for humankind. My opinions mirrored those of Estragon in *Waiting for Godot*: "People are bloody ignorant apes"

(Beckett 9). Seeing people as the problem, I can recall wistfully thinking that a nuclear strike confined to the planet's cities might be a blessing if the collateral damage to nature could be minimized.

Such thoughts resemble the destructive cravings of a necrophile. They rightfully disgust the biophile, but they match the people-as-cancer, disaster-as-cure logic put forth by Earth First! A columnist writing in *Earth First! Journal* under the pseudonym of Miss Ann Thropy once applauded the arrival of Acquired Immune Deficiency Syndrome because "'it only affects humans' and shows promise for wiping out large numbers of them"(Scarce 92). As the columnist states, "'If radical environmentalists were to invent a disease to bring human population back to ecological sanity, it would probably be something like AIDS'" (92). To grasp how one of Brower's biophilic beer drinkers could make so inhumane a statement, we must examine the eco-warriors' goals, which go beyond preservation of wilderness to a reduction of the human masses that would make possible a return to a more ecologically-sound, hunter-gatherer existence (92). Such a lifestyle would support, at best, a few million people. So to reestablish an Eden where a deserving few could coexist with nature, the rest of humanity would have to die. Presumably, only the folk strengthened and purified by nature, the eco-warriors themselves, would inherit paradise.

In their misanthropic vision of utopia, environmentalists parallel other fanatical groups. Psychologists André Haynal, Miklos Molnar, and Gérard de Puymège write that "it seems as if each time civilization gives off a reflection of degradation and despair, movements are born" which promise "an ideal world of happiness" (69). The creation of utopia nearly always requires a "final catastrophe" (58) that will rid the world of enemies and leave an elite to "subjugate . . . those who fail to participate in this . . . movement of redemption" (58). The ideal world cannot exist, of course, despite heroic or horrific efforts on the part of believers, so frustration, anger, and redoubled hate are the inevitable byproducts. Such emotions lead to aggression, and aggression leads to violence against property and persons. Haynal and his coauthors illustrate this theory by citing fanatics ranging from Robespierre to Charles Manson. To bring about their version of paradise, each leader actually set out to exterminate the "aristocracy" and "pigs" that stood in his way. Even movements that begin with life-affirming goals sometimes end with violence. Consider, for instance, the "pro-life" movement whose members have bombed abortion clinics and, more recently, gunned down abortionists.

To my knowledge, no American environmental group has killed a human being for the cause, but as Rik Scarce points out, the trend in monkey wrenching "does appear to be toward more frequent and more extensive destruction"(265). He cites arson attacks on animal experimentation labs and the 1990 Earth Day sabotage of electricity transmission towers in California, which left "90,000 Pacific Gas and Electric customers without power" (266) and vastly increased "the potential for death or injury to those in hospitals, heavy industry, and elsewhere" (266). Scarce also quotes an anonymous eco-warrior who says "the day might come when shooting timber company executives [will] replace monkeywrenching as the most drastic means for saving old-growth trees" (266). Of course, some may join radical environmental groups because ecotage provides them with an avenue through they can express destructive urges while feeling virtuous. And these necrophiles in biophilic clothing may not be entirely conscious that their professed love of nature is merely a veneer.

Those of us who start out as biophiles, though, must undergo drastic changes to make us willing to hurt someone. My own closest brush with environmental vigilantism happened long after my trash collector days, but as a result of them. Camping in Montana, I came quite close to throwing a fisherman into the Blackfoot River to make it easier for him to retrieve his beer cans. My wife led me away, and not quite prepared to commit assault or murder, I let her. To overcome such qualms, Haynal, Molnar, and de Puymège say, a believer's "personal ideals must undergo a split" (59) that allows him or her to inflict (or tolerate) "destruction in the name of the search for [the] ideal world" (52). To ease this split, fanatical groups often characterize nonbelievers as somehow inhuman, vessels of corruption who "'poison the air with their impure breath'"(103).

The problem for most fanatics, especially environmentalists who begin with a strong sense of justice, is their inability to cleanly break with conventional morality. Misanthropes who retain the slightest self-knowledge will sense (consciously or not) that, still human, they are impure and deserve to die with rest of humanity. Attempts to purify themselves must fail. After all, even the most ascetic eco-warrior must eat, drink, wear clothing, and produce poison in the form of bodily waste. Denying their humanity only leads to despair and self-hatred, for by embracing destruction (if only of bulldozers) and death (if only in the abstract), environmentalists take steps toward becoming the necrophilic aliens they intuitively hate—losing their capacity to love the earth or themselves. As Haynal, Molnar, and de Puymège say, "Fanaticism always implies a betrayal of self, which is manifested by an inner anguish—deep, gnawing guilt feelings which cannot be shaken despite attempts to camouflage them through loud protestations and tireless activity" (59).

Faced with a choice between betrayal of themselves or their ideals, some members of the movement may, like Marxist hippies who grow up to sell real estate, abandon the cause altogether and become marketing persons. Some may follow the path of Christopher McCandless, the idealistic former Emory University student who felt strongly enough about world hunger to donate his $20,000 education fund to famine relief (Krakauer 41). Two years later, perhaps remaining true to his extreme ascetic philosophy, McCandless starved to death in the Alaska wilderness. As Scarce shows us, some eco-warriors may even give in to necrophilous urges and take the road to violence and death. In these ways, the environmental movement's misanthropic bent may cost it committed people who, if their love of the earth had not twisted into hate, might have found creative, life-affirming ways to save the planet.

To the original question—Can we learn to love the earth and ourselves?—I have no definite answer except to say we must. Ideological movements that rely on violence do not win the hearts of the uncommitted. Faced with fanatical actions, such as September 11, 2001, the Boston Marathon bombings, and other acts of terror, most people grieve for a while, shake their heads at the illogical acts, and move on, convinced the perpetrators are insane. Rather than try to bomb the uncommitted majority into submission, environmentalists must somehow persuade people to practice an enlightened self-interest, saving the environment to save themselves. The success of any reform movement, Haynal, Molnar, de Puymège say, depends on whether, in envisioning the future world, reformers have taken "factors of reality sufficiently into account" (69). If our vision "is completely utopian and unreal, the result of a purely paranoid projection distorting the perception of reality, it runs the risk of actually contributing to the destruction of the society" (69).

So rather than grasp at radical, misanthropic solutions, such as the decimation of humanity and a return to a hunter-gatherer economy, perhaps we need to take a loving, clear-eyed look at ourselves and the world. If we cannot rebuild Eden, how much of the original paradise can we still save, how much can we reclaim, and what habits, customs, or conveniences will we have to give up so wilderness *and* civilization can thrive? When we can answer these questions, perhaps we can act as a nation, even a species, to achieve a workable balance. As Scarce suggests, "What is needed . . . are constructive suggestions, not death wishes" (93-4). I propose we begin by letting go of the misanthropy that, too often, leads not to joy and growth, but to misery and death. Fromm seconds this motion, saying, "the increase of antinecrophilous tendencies is the one hope we have that the great experiment, *Homo sapiens*, will not fail . . . . The forces working against it are formidable and there is no reason for optimism. But I believe there is reason for hope" (398).

My own period of intense misanthropy ended in my early thirties, with the birth of my first son. Despite the disposable diapers, which resurrected unpleasant memories of my trash collecting days, he gave me something Brower could not. In his face I found hope for the future—and rekindled motivation to do what I can to save what's left of the wilderness, so that he too can taste its beauty and freedom. As he reminded me, people may be bloody ignorant apes, but they have a natural beauty all their own.

Works Cited

Abbey, Edward. *Desert Solitaire: A Season in the Wilderness*. New York: Ballantine, 1968. Print.

---. *Hayduke Lives!* New York: Little, 1990. Print.

---. *The Monkey Wrench Gang*. New York: Avon, 1975. Print.

Brown, Barbara B., and Douglas D. Perkins. "Disruptions in Place Attachment." *Place Attachment*. Ed. Irwin Altman and Setha M. Low. New York: Plenum, 1992. 279-304. Print.

Fromm, Erich. *The Anatomy of Human Destructiveness*. New York: Holt, 1973. Print.

Haynal, André, Miklos Molnar, and Gérard de Puymège. *Fanaticism: A Historical and Psychoanalytical Study*. Trans. Linda Butler Koseoglu. New York: Schocken, 1983. Print.

Krakauer, Jon. "Death of an Innocent: How Christopher McCandless Lost His Way in the Wilds." *Outside* Jan. 1993: 38+. Print.

McPhee, John. *Encounters with the Archdruid*. New York: Farrar, 1971. Print.

Scarce, Rik. *Eco-warriors: Understanding the Radical Environmental Movement*. Chicago: Noble, 1990. Print.

Present with Counsel

We're two hours from the Williamson County Justice Center, driving south along Interstate 35, when Nathan tells me to stop worrying. He has a foolproof method of purging THC from his system. "Besides, I haven't smoked in a couple of weeks, so I'm clean."

The THC remedy involves drinking large quantities of vinegar mixed with lemon juice and downing mega-doses of niacin.

This disclosure explains details that have, until now, puzzled me: First, the number of times Nathan has asked me to stop at gas stations and McDonald's restaurants along our route. Second, the deep scarlet of his complexion—an apparent side-effect of niacin overdose. Third, his self-assurance as we draw closer to a courtroom presided over by the state's toughest DWI judge.

"So you think some concoction you found on the Internet is going to help you beat Williamson County's drug test?"

"Trust me, Dad. I've used it lots of times to pass the drug tests at work. They're negative every time."

I feel a sharp pain, no doubt from the peptic ulcer that began perforating my stomach lining the previous July, when a state trooper arrested Nathan for speeding, driving while intoxicated, and possession of marijuana not long after Nathan started home from a sales job in Austin. Nathan called my house at three o'clock on a Sunday morning. His stepmother Julie answered the phone, shook me half awake, and handed me the receiver.

"Dad? I'm in jail in Georgetown, twenty miles outside Austin. You need to bail me out."

Still half-blind and groggy from sleep, I jotted down the number to the Williamson County Jail and said I'd call in the morning. Having never bailed anyone out of jail, I had no idea where to begin. I also had no idea what to do about Nathan, a bright, witty young man on an up-and-down thrill ride since early high school. As I told him during the short call the deputies permitted us later that morning, "Maybe I should let you sit in jail for a few days to learn a lesson."

"You don't know what you're talking about," Nathan shouted over the phone. "It's horrible in this place. Please don't abandon me."

Steve Sherwood

As Julie and I discussed the best thing to do, I tested the waters with my ex-wife, who insisted we bail him out right away. "But aren't we just making him dependent if we keep helping him?" I asked. "I can't believe he keeps fucking up like this."

"So our oldest son's a fuck-up and a loser? Is that what you're saying?"

I shook my head as if she could see me through the phone line. "I said he's fucking up, not that he's a fuck-up. I love him but I'm also disappointed, which leaves us right where we started. I'll talk things over with Julie and get back to you."

Julie consulted an attorney friend, who settled the matter. "Get him out of there as soon as you can," the friend said. "Nothing good comes from spending time in a Texas jail, and he could rot there for weeks before a hearing."

A bored Williamson County deputy gave me almost no information about Nathan's case beyond the statutory fines for each offense (a total of $3,500). He likewise offered no advice on bail other than to suggest I contact a local bail bondsman. During another call, I spoke to Nathan long enough to reassure him that we would bail him out, but he might have to stay there for another night. He sounded bad, on the verge of tears.

"You have no idea what it's like in here."

"I'm sorry, son. I wish you didn't have to go through this. Hang in there for another day, and we'll have you out by tomorrow morning."

Taking no chances, Nathan phoned his own bail bondsman (or bondswoman), who put together a conference call with me and my ex to negotiate the ransom. To spring him, we would each have to put up $2,200, of which the bonding company would return only $1,750 when Nathan entered a plea. We gave the woman our credit card numbers over the phone. She would take it from there.

I planned to take Monday off work to fetch Nathan from jail, but my ex said some of his co-workers, who like him sold bundles of TV, Internet, and telephone services door-to-door, would pick him up Monday afternoon on their return trip from Austin to Fort Worth. As neither of us knew, the state trooper who busted Nathan had ordered his car towed to Round Rock, ten miles south of Georgetown, and left his valuables in the trunk. So when Williamson Country cut Nathan loose, he had no identification, credit cards, cash, keys, or phone. Hungry, parched, and

66

technically a vagrant, with no visible means of support, he wandered the streets of Georgetown for six hours until his co-workers found him.

As the stern father who balked at bailing out his son, I took the brunt of Nathan's anger. The first time we saw each other after the arrest, he confronted me about my careless words.

"You think I'm a fuck-up and a loser." His expression, raw and wounded, made him look younger than his twenty-three years.

I fumbled for an explanation. "That's not what I said, Nathan, but I'm sorry because I did say some things I regret. You seemed to be doing so well at the new job and—"

"I *am* doing well," he shouted. "Why can't you just be proud of what I do right instead of calling me a loser and a fuck-up whenever I make a mistake?"

I took a deep breath and let it out. "I don't know."

The truth hung with the dust in the air between us. Against all reason, I still clung to hopes raised by the talents and potential he showed as a child. A lack-luster school performance and behavior problems soon dampened these hopes. Each year, teachers would laud Nathan's creativity, sense of humor, and intelligence. Within a few weeks, angry e-mails about missing homework and disrespectful behavior would start coming in.

The divorce didn't help matters. He was eleven when his mother left, and after I met and married Julie, we did what we could for him, including encouragement, tough love, and medication for ADHD, with which a psychologist had finally diagnosed him at age sixteen. A fast reader, an excellent writer, and an intuitive mathematician, he scored better on the Scholastic Aptitude Test than anyone in his family, including his college professor father, but his average grades kept him out of the university where I work, and which he could have attended free of charge. At a local community college, he majored in marijuana and Halo until asked to leave at the end of his freshman year. Having spent all my savings on his room and board, I suggested he find a job to support himself. For two years, he not only worked at Sam's Club but also managed to earn an associate's degree in liberal arts at another community college. He met a girl, fell in love, and moved into an apartment with her. Then, just as life started looking good, a cash register error cost him his job.

This setback led to others, including the loss of his apartment and girlfriend. My ex and I had urged him to look for another job before the rent came due. He told us we worried too much. If no one offered him work, he said, he could always become a stand-up comedian or a Zen street philosopher, trading words of wisdom for handouts from strangers.

Worried despite such assurances, we told him not to plan on staying in either of our homes. Julie and I had already raised and dismissed the possibility of taking him in when he lost his job. The smoking and drinking would set a poor example for his younger brother and step-sisters. But our starkest fear was that if we took him in, he would become a guest-room squatter—pretending to hunt for a job while conducting endless campaigns of Grand Theft Auto and posting anti-establishment rants on Ron Paul blogs. At one point, a week before he became homeless, I called to tell him about an ad for a railroad job that paid fifteen bucks an hour and had benefits.

Nathan laughed at the notion. "Why would I want to work outside in the Texas heat? I'm holding out for an office job."

A few days later, still without any job prospects, he confided to me his deep fear that no one would hire someone so recently fired by Sam's Club.

"A lot of people lose their jobs," I told him. "They can't let a single setback stop them from finding work again, and neither can you."

Instead of searching for a job, Nathan sat in his apartment until the lease ran out. Then he phoned to ask if he could spend the night. "Mom won't let me stay with her, so I have no place to sleep except my car. Scott and Julie's girls get to stay with you, so why can't I come home too?"

"They're still in school—that's the difference. We love you as much as we love them, but we just can't take you in."

My words sounded lame and hollow in the receiver, as they no doubt did to him, and I felt myself weakening. Images of Nathan at all ages came to me, as they often did when I saw or spoke to him. The dark-haired baby with the searching smile morphed into the proud eight-year-old receiving his blue belt in karate, who morphed into the sullen, smirking teen in black jeans and heavy metal t-shirts, who morphed into the young man with the sideburns and soul patch, still deeply in love with the girl who left him. I wanted to say, "Sure, honey, come on home." Instead, I held firm, hung up the phone, and broke down in tears.

For two weeks, my ex and I split the cost of a pay-by-the-week motel room for Nathan. Just as the two weeks were almost up, he found a job stocking shelves for Wal-Mart five nights a week. The hours, from 11 p.m. to 7 a.m., were brutal, and not conducive to a social life, but the wages did cover his rent and other expenses. He kept the job for more than a year before becoming a salesman, work for which he had a natural flare.

Then came the DWI and possession bust.

Now, in spite of six restroom stops, we reach Georgetown with enough time for lunch at Chili's, which is three miles from the justice center. I order a Caribbean chicken salad. Before vanishing into the men's room, Nathan asks me to order him a burger, fries, and a Coke. By the time the food arrives, he has been in the restroom for fifteen minutes, and I'm starting to worry. Hungry, I eat without him and am about to mount a search party when he comes to the table looking ill, his face niacin-overdose scarlet beneath the thick brown hair, eyebrows, and soul patch.

"Can you eat?"

He takes a small bite of the burger before pushing it away. "I don't think so."

"Better go, then."

The Williamson County Justice Center, familiar now after three preliminary hearings, is one of the larger buildings in Georgetown, housing eight courtrooms and related clerk and probation offices. We know the drill now and remove belts and other possessions from our clothes for the trip through the metal detectors. I give Nathan the once-over as we make our way to the doors of the courtroom. He looks handsome in a suit—like any other young professional—but he has no socks on under the black loafers, something I should have noticed before now. He had his often-chaotic hair cut short for the occasion and he has no visible tattoos or piercings, which separates him from the other defendants. Also, thanks perhaps to a residual glow from the niacin or to the fluorescent lights of the Justice Center, his complexion looks healthy, unlike the dark gray of the serious drinkers we find in the courtroom.

The bailiff, a strongly built Latino with a wide, pleasant face and an easy smile, reminds everyone in the courtroom to tuck in his or her shirt, to find an empty seat, to stand if called upon, and to add "your honor" after answering the judge's questions.

In the gallery sit several defendants I've seen at past hearings: a sandy haired man with large ear gauges, a heavily tattooed woman in jeans and a t-shirt holding hands with a young blonde in a dress; a Latino man in carefully ironed ranch clothes; an older woman in a low-cut blouse, whose mouths twists as if in agony and whose puffy eyes drizzle tears; an African American man in a tasteful, understated purple suit; a rangy young white kid accompanied by five family members, including his one-eyed grandmother, who reaches over often to pat his back and say she loves him. We sit among them and a dozen other defendants, who like Nathan, wait to hear the judge decree their fate. Nathan looks cool and confident, though his hand trembles as he raises it to brush his hair.

In terms of appearance, the attorneys vary as much as their clients. One young lawyer has slicked-back hair and a Robert Downey Junior smirk. Another is a middle-aged Latina in high heels and a dress that shows off a spectacular figure. There are old, fat attorneys, too, but all of them have two things in common: They are better dressed than their clients and they look relaxed and happy.

Nathan's attorney, David, finds us before court goes into session and leads us into the tiled corridor to talk. He's younger than I, maybe early forties, with short blond hair. Trim, energetic, businesslike, David has a smile that crinkles his eyes.

"Well, here we go," he says and his eyes crinkle. He passes Nathan a sheaf of papers to read and sign. "You blew under the legal limit, so the DWI is off the table. You'll plead guilty to reckless driving and do a deferred adjudication for the possession charge. That means you'll serve fifteen months' probation and pay court costs and fines. Stick to the terms, and the possession charge will go away at the end of probation. All you have to do now is pass the drug test."

"No problem," Nathan says.

David searches his face. "That's good because the whole deal hinges on it. If you test positive, the judge can send you straight to jail for a hundred and eighty days."

"No problem."

An officer of the court—a tall, thin older man with a gray crew cut and a grim face—will come for Nathan when it is his turn to pee in a cup. Meanwhile, we return to the courtroom for the roll call. The judge enters a few minutes later. All of us, defendants in the gallery and a dozen attorneys gathered near the defense table, stand until she sits at the bench. A thin, pleasant-looking woman with long, brown hair, the judge has a narrow face with a down-turned mouth and mournful eyes. She does not look like the toughest DWI judge in Texas, but that's the rumor.

She reads the names of the defendants, who stand up and say, "Here, your honor." Their attorney, if they have one, echoes this reply with "Present with counsel."

Those who fail to answer forfeit their bond. Today is the fourth time that, by arriving in time for roll call, we have rescued the $4,400 Nathan's mother and I put up in exchange for his liberty.

Once the roll call ends, the hearings begin. David comes for Nathan and waves me back to my seat. I'm not sure what's going on, but while they're gone the judge sentences the young man with the one-eyed grandmother, the woman with the puffy face and twisted mouth, the African American man in the purple suit, and four other defendants, including the woman with the tattoos, to jail time. The judge issues these sentences in a soft, kindly voice, and with each case, the painful knot in my stomach tightens another notch.

After more than an hour, David fetches me. In the corridor, with an abashed smile, he says, "Nathan's having a hard time. We're still waiting for him to fill the cup."

I let out my breath. "I'm so proud."

David laughs. "Nathan's not my typical client. He seems like a great guy—funny and smart, with lots of potential."

"Yes he is, and he has a good heart, but he tends to sabotage himself. He could have gone to my university for free—and he had excellent SAT and ACT scores—but during high school he seldom turned in his homework."

A short laugh, more like a cough, hurts my throat. "I think he set a school record by flunking algebra three times. He usually got the answers right, but he refused to show his work, so the teachers gave him half the points."

"Well, let's hope he did his homework this time."

His homework, assigned by the judge at his last hearing, was to stay drug free from that moment until today. I give an absent nod, recalling the many rest stops between Fort Worth and Georgetown.

For another hour, as David and I sit on a bench in the hallway, I remember when Nathan was in second grade and had to visit the principal's office for the third time in a week. That night, he claimed he had done nothing to deserve punishment: he had tossed a ball of paper back at a kid who threw it at him. I suggested that maybe his past misbehaviors were coming back to hurt him even though he was trying to be good now. He agreed and said, "It's like I'm a little boat being tossed on the waves. The waves are the past and the dock is the future, and I can't get to the dock no matter what I do." I held out my arms to him, and said, "Come here, Little Boat." We hugged.

He got in trouble again the next day.

The door to the men's room opens, and the court officer with the gray hair and the grim expression exits with a specimen sample, pauses in front of David, and shakes his head.

Nathan follows him out, still adjusting his sport coat. "That can't be right. Something's definitely wrong with your test."

The older man raises his eyebrows but makes no reply. I'm not sure whether to swear or cry, so I close my eyes for a moment to shut out the sight of Nathan, whose brown eyes are round with shock and the stark probability that he's about to do time.

As the older man returns to the courtroom with the test results, David faces us. "Well, this is not good news. Our deferred adjudication deal is off the table. The options are either simple probation, which means the possession conviction stays on your record, or six months in jail. It's up to the judge."

Only half a dozen spectators remain in the once-full gallery. The smiling bailiff escorts Nathan to the jury benches, on the judge's left, where three other defendants with positive drug tests await sentencing. Nathan sits next to a young black man with a Nike swoosh carved into the hair above one ear and watches as the judge sentences the other defendants—a young Latina and an older white man who looks like an indigent—to ninety days. Relatives in the gallery moan or dab at tears. Nathan folds his hands before him, as if he's praying, and for the first time today his face looks pale beneath the dark hair. His eyes—brave yet devoid of hope—meet mine for an instant, and suddenly I'm light-headed, scarcely able to breathe. An image of Nathan at age eleven, wearing the t-shirt he earned by completing his fifth grade drug abuse resistance education program, returns to mock me. Nathan swore that day never to experiment with any drug, including alcohol. That was before he tried his drug of choice, of course, before he came to need marijuana simply to calm him enough to fall asleep at night.

As I lean heavily against the bench in front of me, the young man with the Nike swoosh gets a hundred and eighty days for possession. To keep fear at bay, I think about practical things: what to do with Nathan's car, clothes, computer, furniture, and other possessions while he's in custody. Whether I or his mother can break the lease on his apartment and shut off the power and water. Someone will have to contact his sales

manager, I think, but I don't know the man's name. And God kn
Nathan will do for work six months from now with a convicti
record.

David asks to approach the bench, and he and the judge
whispers for several minutes as Nathan sits with his eyes ca
search the judge's face for signs of mercy, and she startles m
scanning my face with her mournful eyes.

The whispers continue until David leaves the judge's b
through the gate into the gallery, and leans down to talk to
come down here for every hearing and you teach at a univ
judge is willing to give Nathan one last chance. Promise to gi
the way back to Fort Worth, and she'll grant him five weeks
together enough to pass the drug test. If he fails again, he
inside for six months. If he passes, he'll get the deferred adju

Already grieving for my son, I stare at David. "Is that
"It's the best we can do."

That's not what I mean, I start to say. But now is
question the justice of giving a white kid, the son of a coll
second chance after so many other kids, mostly black and
gone to jail for the same offense. I can agonize over ethic
social justice once Nathan is safely, if temporarily, out of r
"Yes, of course. Tell her I'll be happy to chastise him al
Worth."

Later, when Nathan leaves the justice center, pale
him. "Do you know how close you came today to going
He closes his eyes and nods. "I've never been so
"Me either. Remember how it feels. If you fail an
deserve whatever sentence the judge gives you."

He pushes me away. "I'm not stupid. You think
jail?"

I regard him calmly. "You have no right to be
told the judge I'd give you hell all the way home, and
to do. Get ready for it."

But halfway to Waco, I run out of hell. Nath
sounds sincere—to give up marijuana and find and
at night. I suggest Tylenol PM. Later, hoping to say
him we need to discuss something. He looks at m
know I hurt you two summers ago when I would

hurt me almost as much to turn you away, and I want to say I'm sorry. ou're my son. I love you and I *am* proud of you. I hope someday you'll nderstand why I thought I had to do it."

Nathan puts a hand on my shoulder. "I know, Dad. It's okay. To tell u the truth, if you'd let me come home, I wouldn't have taken the night at Wal-Mart, which means I wouldn't have met Phil, who turned me on the sales job. Of course, if I hadn't taken the sales job, I wouldn't have n driving through Williamson County last summer, so—"

"So this whole mess is my fault?"

He smiles. "Well, maybe just a fraction."

"I guess I can live with that."

For a short time, there's a peace between us, an uncomplicated itude simply to be together, to be free, to be driving away from trouble.

I spot a billboard for the Cracker Barrel at the next exit. "Hungry?"

Nathan groans. "You must be reading my mind. I'm half-starved."

"Let's eat."

Keepsakes

Sarah's brothers stepped down from combine and grain truck and brushed wheat chaff out of their dark hair. Sarah threw an arm around each of their necks. Looking bone tired behind paper masks that filtered out enough dust to let them work the harvest, they broke her embrace to use aerosol devices that shot medication into their lungs. Then the older of the two, Lane, came over to shake my hand, doing a little bow as if to apologize for his six feet seven inches of bony angles.

I offered to shake with Rhys, shorter and heavier than Lane, until he showed me the oil on his hands.

"What brings you to Kansas?" Lane asked.

"Didn't your mother tell you? We're here to help with the harvest."

A look passed between my brothers-in-law, and they bent to examine the combine's broken drive chain.

"There must be something we can do to make your jobs easier," I said into the silence.

A master mechanic, Rhys patted the combine. "Know what makes one of these tick?"

I looked at the tangle of machinery, half the size of our apartment in Colorado. "My first guess would be a big engine."

They shared the look again, faces impassive. Lane nodded at the worn, two-story farmhouse, neglected in the nine months since their father died and their mother moved to town. "If you like, you can mow the weeds in the yard."

He had to show me how to operate the riding mower, whose engine complained under my weight. I tried to catch Sarah's eye but couldn't. At the time, she still hoped to reform me in the image of her male relatives, any one of whom, blindfolded, could rebuild a Chevy.

During the courtship, our first fight had come when I insisted on having my Subaru serviced. "We never take our cars to the shop," she'd said. "Dad does all the repairs himself."

"Well, I'm not your father."

"No."

"And I don't want to be."

"Don't worry," she'd said.

Now I mowed a forest of goldenrod, sending her brothers scrambling for their breathers. Long before I finished, they climbed back into their vehicles and drove away. Sarah came over and made a slashing motion across her throat. I cut the engine, and she said, "Sorry, honey, but the boys don't need our help."

"So I gathered," I said, surprised at the depth of my disappointment. Pulling together as a family to harvest Graham Robert's wheat, planted in the weeks before he died, had become important to me somehow.

"You would have loved harvest in the old days," Sarah said. "We used to ride in the combine with Dad; Mom cooked and drove the grain trucks. The house was filled with people."

She looked at the homestead—empty but for the few rooms Lane occupied, then out across the fields that stretched to the horizon, the earth that supported the Roberts family for three generations swept into a distant, chocolate-colored dust devil.

"The boys know we want to help, and mowing the yard reminded Lane of the southwest quarter," she said. "So tomorrow we'll take the tractors out and cut weeds in the fallow fields."

I was tense that evening in my mother-in-law's backyard because she was spraying Raid at the bugs that flew over the barbecue.

"Do you think you should do that?" I asked.

If I'd used her name, I might have stopped her, but we were on a "hey" basis. A year ago, when Sarah announced our wedding plans, Graham had welcomed me to the family with a smile and a hug, but Sarah's mother showed the idea little warmth. Now, I felt uncomfortable calling her Hannah or Mom, and *Mrs. Roberts* rang too formal. So I said, "Hey, are you sure you want to eat Raid?" as the horseflies and mosquitoes crash-landed on our burgers.

Sarah's glance cut through the smoke and insecticide to warn that our marriage of ten months might last longer if I said no more. I joined her paternal grandmother, Electa, who sat nearby and watched Hannah with a critical expression. The family matriarch, Electa had a deceptively soft voice that could harden abruptly. She tightly controlled most of the land Graham had farmed, in part, according to Sarah, because she never took to her daughter-in-law. From the occasional sparks between them, I gathered the feeling was mutual.

Electa turned to me. "You know, Sarah was the homecoming queen, the prettiest girl in the county. We always figured she'd find herself a farmer and settle down here."

"Mmmm," I replied. Instead, she escaped and married me. I glanced at Sarah, whose dark-haired, Midwestern good looks drew me to her, and whose loyalty to family and quiet strength of will made loving her inevitable. We hardly had time to get to know one another before Graham died and a small, undefinable part of Sarah drew away from me. "Hard to figure, isn't she?"

Lane and Rhys came in from the fields to eat the poisoned burgers with wolfish gratitude, nodding or shaking their heads at the women's questions without stopping to talk. Electa brooded as they ate, finally blurting out, "Young people don't appreciate farming anymore. It's a good life if you're willing to work. Your father knew that."

Still chewing, the brothers avoided her eyes, which shone beneath her bifocals with the hint of tears. "After supper, I'm going to the cemetery," Electa said. "Who'll come along?"

Hannah and the boys agreed to go, but I stopped in mid-nod when Sarah said, "I believe I'll stay here."

Electa's face darkened. "Your mother says you haven't visited the grave since the funeral."

I recalled that day as a blur of sympathetic expressions and homemade pies. Sarah wore a fixed smile as she passed the open casket and Hannah said, "Well, don't he look nice. They even waxed his mustache." Since then, Sarah had refused to discuss Graham's death even with me.

"I'm staying here," she said now. "You all go on ahead."

"Maybe your mother has something to say about showing respect for the dead," Electa said.

But tending a new batch of hamburgers at the barbecue, Hannah only frowned and gave the bugs another shot of Raid.

Dust marked Sarah's position in the next field. Earlier, as Lane explained my tractor's controls, Sarah climbed aboard hers and checked the gauges like a pro.

"Nothing to it," Lane said. "Drives like a car, except you use the brakes to make sharp turns like a tank. Oh, and the throttle is beside the steering wheel and you need to raise your undercutting blades before you back up. Got it?"

"You mean those things?"

He clapped me on the shoulder. "You'll do fine."

Now Sarah was making orderly passes, leaving a wake of disturbed earth and slashed weeds. I mimicked her, settling into an uneasy rhythm, warmed when a passing trucker mistook me for a farmer and waved.

In choosing our vehicles, Sarah had presented me with the old tractor as if bestowing a gift of love. "It was the first in the county with air conditioning," she said. "It's Dad's favorite."

Her use of the present tense worried me. Did she know what she was saying? Should I confront her? I wondered. But when she talked about Graham, she looked so happy and so fragile I didn't dare. And in a way, she was right. His imprint was everywhere: in the arrangement of outbuildings, in the choice of equipment, in the shape of the fields. He was a big man, an inch or two over six feet and close to 260 pounds. As I drove, feeling the engine's heavy throb, I sat in the hollow he'd left in the seat cushion, not quite filling it. At our wedding, he had crushed my hand. "You take care of my Sarah," he said, and he didn't let go till I swore I would. The next time we shook, he couldn't speak. Sarah flew to Kansas, and I drove all night to be with her. By the time I arrived, though, she had done her crying and seemed resigned, almost cheerful, in spite of the septic smell of the cancer ward.

The tractor drove more or less like a car, as Lane said, and after cutting weeds for most of the morning, I felt I was mastering the controls. Then, as I cranked the steering wheel into a tight left turn for another pass, the tractor's front end seemed to sink into the field. The powerful rear wheels churned and the engine compartment plowed a furrow. When the entire vehicle tipped to one side and threatened to roll, I cut the engine and jumped out.

The tractor leaned at an extreme angle, its front wheel assembly jammed under the rear wheels. I circled, bending to examine the snapped steering column.

"Christ, what have I done?" I muttered.

Why hadn't Lane warned me that I couldn't make a sharp turn without losing the front end? With a dreadful feeling that maybe he had, I sat on the hot dirt. Sarah found me there. Sunbaked, I passively watched her climb from her tractor and kneel beside me.

"Are you all right?"

"I'm sorry, honey," I said.

She studied the wreck of Graham's favorite tractor for a while and then leaned her forehead against my shoulder.

We sat in a grain truck at the edge of a rolling wheat field. "Forget it," Lane said. "It's my fault for not doing the maintenance. If Dad was here, it wouldn't have happened."

I drank some water that tasted faintly of aluminum and went back to watching Rhys work. A grain-reaping maestro, he cut wheat for hours at a stretch, grim behind his filter mask. Lane drove to the local elevator whenever Rhys filled one of the haul trucks. Meanwhile, I played water boy or sometimes Lane let me drive, but we all knew I was nothing but ballast.

"It wasn't your fault," Lane repeated.

I looked up at him. "Has Sarah ever talked to you about your dad?" He frowned slightly, and I added, "About his death, I mean."

"No need to," he said slowly. "We know how they felt about each other. He loved us all, but he loved Sarah best. You might have noticed, Mom's not much for hugging and kissing and all. She handed out the punishment and the religion. Hugging and kissing and comforting—that was Dad's job."

"Whose job is it now?" I asked.

The question seemed to surprise him. "Nobody's, I guess."

Rhys drove up then and sent a stream of grain shooting through a curved auger into the truck's bed. Over the noise, Lane shouted, "You and Sarah are lucky to have somebody."

After a while, I shouted back, "You dating anyone?"

He actually blushed. "You don't meet anybody stuck out here on the farm."

"I guess not."

"I'm no good with women anyhow," he added. "Too tall."

"Maybe you haven't met the right one."

"How did you know Sarah was right for you?"

I thought for a long time, unable to come up with an answer I could feel sure he'd understand. Finally, I shrugged. "The way she looked at me, I guess."

At the top of a low hill, a mile from town, a square of green lay among the ripe wheat fields. People drove here to sit in the dark and watch lightning storms, Sarah said. Families gathered on Decoration Day to spruce up the graves of ancestors, and one could nearly always find a loyal widow paying respects.

Sarah did not explain her decision to visit the cemetery, saying only that she wanted my company. From the funeral, I tried to recall whether Graham's grave lay under the trees or out in the open, but the headstones cast long shadows in the fading sunlight and everything looked different to me.

Earlier, Hannah had retrieved Sarah from the fallow fields and brought us lunch, spreading the food out on the tailgate of her pickup. Sarah and her brothers ate and talked of other harvests, other tailgate lunches. Slapping baloney slices onto white bread, Rhys laughed and said, "Dad sure loved his baloney. Remember? Just like this, with lots of mayo." Maybe Sarah saw something in her mother's face. Anyway, she went over and put her arms around Hannah's neck, only to back away when Hannah's body stiffened at the touch.

"Well then," Hannah muttered, turning away. "I'll be getting back to town."

It took us an hour to find Graham's headstone. We stood looking down at the marker, silently reading and rereading his name.

"It's like I thought," Sarah finally said. "He's not here."

I looked at her.

"I don't know where he is, but he's not here."

By the end of the week, Lane and Rhys had brought in all but twenty-five acres of Graham's wheat. "Three or four hours' work and we'll be done," Lane said. "If you like, you can head for home in the morning."

Having finished the weeding, Sarah sat between us in a pair of cut-offs, her bare leg resting against mine. I watched her pop a handful of raw wheat into her mouth.

"You're not eating that," I said.

"It turns to gum if you chew it long enough."

I glanced at Lane, who nodded. "Dad taught us."

Sarah's jaw muscles bunched as she chewed. "See?" She opened her lips to show a wad of blond gum plastered against her teeth, then startled me by blowing a bubble. "Want some?"

"I don't think so."

"You can have some of mine," she offered and smiled in a way I hadn't seen for a long time. We moved closer together.

Lane watched us with an exasperated look. "You two want to cut that out?"

Later, Sarah said, "Lane, Grandma says you're going to quit farming."

Lane was silent for so long, I wasn't sure he would reply. Finally, he said. "Wasn't for Dad, I never would've kept at it so long. What I'm really interested in is computers."

"How about Rhys?"

"He can't stand the dust."

"What's going to happen to the farm?"

"Jake Hocklemier tried to buy Mom and Grandma out a week after Dad died," he said. "He's gobbling up the county at bargain prices—mostly from widows with medical bills, like Mom."

"Will he get our land?"

"If he's patient."

Sarah left us and waded out into the wheat. I followed, meaning to comfort her, but when I touched her shoulder she surprised me by smiling up at me.

"I used to gallop Princess across this field in the spring," she said. "The wheat grass was soft on her hooves, and it always made me feel so free. Dad knew we were trampling the crop and costing him money, but he never stopped me."

We waded deeper into the shoulder-high stalks. Finally, she said, "I'm going to miss him."

Rhys drove by in the combine, spewing chaff into the air. The wind caught it and blew it back in our faces as we walked to the truck. From the cab we watched him mow down what was left of the wheat, leaving stubble and bare ground. Within three hours, twenty-five acres of wheat became three loads of grain, which we took turns driving to the elevator.

On the last trip, as we waited to dump our load, Sarah got out and filled a small jar with wheat. She looked embarrassed as she slipped it into her purse.

"Just a keepsake," she said.

Marathon

The trouble started in a small Mexican village when a pig gored Aldo Springer in the ass.

A single-hole outhouse served as the village's public toilet, and instead of falling into a deep pit, Springer's droppings hit the packed dirt of the village square. Springer was sitting there, wondering how the villagers kept the space beneath the toilet so clean when the pig—a walking honey wagon—came in through a trapdoor and gored him before gobbling up its latest meal.

Everyone laughed when Springer left the outhouse at a run, his jeans around his knees. The villagers, his fellow backpackers, his fiancée Lisa Jablonski, and Jason Mauser, the former Outward Bound instructor who was leading the group through Copper Canyon—everyone laughed. Out of embarrassment, Springer pulled up his pants. Out of pain, he hobbled around, waiting for the throb of torn tissue and nerve endings to subside. Out of anger, he looked for an ax or machete. And all the time the pig stood beside the outhouse and watched him with its amber grin. Only when the blood that poured down the back of Springer's leg filled his hiking boot, and he left dark, sodden boot prints in the packed dirt, did Lisa stop laughing.

"Jesus, Aldo, you're hurt," she said.

Lisa had rounded cheekbones, brown eyes shot with green and gold specks, and a wide, delicately curved mouth. Her short blonde hair showed off a long, muscular neck that at quieter moments Springer liked to nuzzle. A certified public accountant who worked for the Boulder office of a national accounting firm, Lisa had the lean body of a marathoner. She knew something about first aid, so Springer asked her to look at his wound.

"Let's get you out of the square first," she said. "Lean on me."

They did a three-legged race out of the village. A pack of young boys in white shirts and shorts, tire-tread sandals, and straw cowboy hats chased them. The boys pointed at Springer and grunted like pigs. Lisa led the parade beyond a series of adobe walls, through an avocado orchard, to a thicket of willows beside the river, where, except the boys, they had some privacy. From her backpack, Lisa took out a Johnson & Johnson first-aid kit. She told Springer to drop his jeans, an act that brought discussion and more grunts from the boys.

A stab of pain told Springer when Lisa found the wound. She drew in her breath. "This is bad, Aldo, a lot worse than I thought. You'll need stitches. And antibiotics."

"How deep is it?"

There was another sudden stab of pain. "I don't know," she said and stood up. "Deep."

Springer peered into Lisa's eyes as if he might read what she was thinking in the arrangement of the green and gold flecks. Copper Canyon was home to the Tarahumaras, Lisa's idols since childhood. The greatest long distance runners in the world, the Tarahumaras held out against the Spaniards longer than any other Mexican tribe. On the road to Batopilas, Lisa and Springer had caught their first glimpse of a Tarahumara. As the truck carrying the backpacking party labored in low gear up a steep mountain road, a woman with a child on her back passed the truck at an easy lope. The woman, who wore tire-tread sandals, a white cotton blouse, and matching pantaloons, waited at the top of the hill, meeting the wide-eyed gaze of the tourists with a stony expression, dark eyes glinting beneath her black hair. Then she ran on. Lisa watched the woman with the same expression— eyes round, elegant neck arched as she tilted her head to one side— that she wore whenever she reminisced about the year she qualified for the Boston Marathon and stood close enough to the starting line to glimpse Joan Benoit Samuelson. At Batopilas, the truck had dropped off their party, along with the gear they would need for a two-week trek through Copper Canyon. Then the driver turned around and headed back up the winding, cliff-hugging road toward Creel while the backpackers left Batopilas on a trail that hugged the river.

Now, with tape and sterile pads from the first aid kit, Lisa did what she could to close Springer's wound. The young boys gave no sign of going away. And as Springer delicately hitched up his jeans, Jason Mauser came toward them through the avocado orchard. Mauser walked with the smooth, easy stride of an experienced outdoorsman, thigh muscles knotting under the tanned skin of his legs. Dressed in khaki shorts and a faded blue T-shirt, Mauser had sun-bleached hair, pulled back in a ponytail, a dark beard, a strong nose, and calm blue eyes that took on a faintly ironic gleam whenever they stopped on Springer—a tall, angular music professor who specialized in the flügelhorn. Turned on Lisa, Mauser's eyes took on a solemn quality.

"How's our boy?" Mauser asked.

"Not so good," Lisa said. "It's a deep wound, still seeping blood. I'm afraid we'll have to drop out of the party and catch a ride back to Creel."

"Too bad," Mauser said. "I know how much you were looking forward to the trip. And I wasn't bullshitting you about those Tarahumara *compañeros* of mine. As a favor to me, and for a few pesos, I'm sure they'd let you run with them."

Springer read dejection in the curve of Lisa's neck and shoulders.

"There's a doctor, an old buddy of mine, in the next town," Mauser said. "Ernesto trained north of the border, at Baylor, and he's serving his time in the national medical service. Should be able to take care of our boy here, no problem—patch him up and put him back on the trail." The faintly ironic expression returned to his eyes. "That is, if you think you can walk a few miles."

Springer turned to Lisa. "What do you think?"

She hesitated. "Only if you're sure you can make it."

"How many miles?" Springer asked Mauser.

Mauser shrugged. "A few."

The Cobre River—a bright shade of green—rushed below the trail. The party passed over a rickety wooden footbridge, a hundred feet above the river, and stopped to snap photographs of the sight. This part of Copper Canyon resembled the Grand, though the colors were less striking. White sandstone cliffs rose from the river, and the distant gray crags at the canyon rim looked, to a veteran rock climber like Springer, to offer some intriguing routes. Sage and greasewood grew on the slopes above, below, and between the cliffs, and the thick underbrush along the canyon bottom included tall saguaro cactuses. Wildflowers flashed blue and yellow and pink and purple between boulders, and with the half-bored attitude of a tour guide, Mauser pointed to them and gave their English, Spanish, and scientific names. Mauser also alerted them to dangers of the trail—the jaguars that sometimes wandered north from Guatemala, the bushmasters and rattlesnakes coiled in the brush, and the hostile desert plants. One such plant was a barrel-shaped cactus with two-inch needles. Mauser called it a Texas horse-crippler.

"On my last trip a young woman stepped on one of these," he said. "The needles penetrated the sole of her hiking boot, and we had to carry her out."

Springer hobbled at the rear, whistling selections from Chuck Mangione and Aaron Copeland to keep his mind off the pain. He slung his pack over his left shoulder to prevent contact with the wound, which radiated a septic heat. Lisa walked a few paces ahead, her long legs moving with their usual effortless grace. She paused often to look back at him—a show of concern that also conveyed impatience at being held back.

The bleeding had stopped, but the wound throbbed with such force that, on each step, Springer felt as if some phantom boar were embedding its tusks in his ass. This image goaded him along the trail, and for the first few miles he kept the others in sight. Then, lost for a time in a throbbing daze, he looked up the trail to see nothing but sage, rocks, willows, and greasewood.

Springer leaned against a boulder to rest. That's when a group of men came out of the willows along the river. Three of them formed a line across the trail in front of him. The other two took up positions on the trail leading back the way Springer had come. The men wore faded khaki uniform pants and shirts, like former members of the Mexican police, and tire-tread sandals, like the villagers and the Tarahumaras. All but the apparent leader, whose belly dangled over his belt, carried machetes. The leader had a chrome-plated pistol thrust into his belt, just under the overhang of belly.

The leader said something in Spanish. Springer had taken Spanish classes in his undergraduate days, so he still knew his numbers, colors, and vowel sounds, how to conjugate a dozen verbs, and how to say "who," "what," "when," "where," "why," and "how much." He could also greet strangers, ask the location of the library, the town square, the train station, the stadium, and the discotheque, where he could order a Negro Modelo. Even so, he had no idea what the man with the pistol in his belt was saying.

"¿Que?" Springer asked.

The men on the trail in front of him looked at each other. One of them, a thin man missing his front teeth, repeated Springer's question in mocking tones. The leader spoke again. Springer shook his head and said, "No comprendo."

"No entiende," the thin, toothless man corrected.

The leader drew the chrome-plated pistol. He pointed it first at Springer's nose and then at his backpack, wagging the barrel slightly. This gesture cut through the language barrier. Springer let his pack fall to the trail. One of the men standing behind him took the pack, which held most of what Springer had brought with him to Mexico—clothing, tent, sleeping bag, sleeping pad, cooking gear, camp stove, fuel, water bottles, books, sheet music, condoms. The pack also held Springer's share of the communal food, supplied by Mauser. The leader shifted the pistol barrel to Springer's belt and wagged it again, which Springer interpreted as a command to empty his pockets. He did so, while the man who took the pack went through the outside pouches and came up with the condoms, green aluminum envelopes of Trojans, which he thrust into the air with an exultant cry.

A train of pack mules rounded a bend in the trail. The mules, tended by a man and a boy, were headed away from the village of the pig, in the same direction as Springer. Both the man and boy carried old military rifles, from World War II or the Korean War. As soon as the mule train came into view, the bandits backed into the brush beside the trail, dragging Springer's backpack with them.

Freed of the weight of his pack, Springer moved with a floating sensation up the trail. For half a mile, fueled by nerves, he stayed ahead of the mule train. But gradually, the mules, laden with dusty canvas bags filled with boxes of canned goods, cases of beer, and sacks of flour, drew even with Springer. The man with the rifle nodded a wary greeting. Springer stepped to one side to let the train pass, but as the last mule went by, he threw out a hand and caught one of the wooden knobs on the pack frame, letting the mule pull him along the trail. The boy shouted and waved his rifle. The man stopped the lead mule, and came back to look at Springer with a somber expression.

"*Señor*," the man began. The rest of his sentence came in rapid Spanish, but the gist, Springer suspected, was "Please let go of my mule, gringo."

"*Por favor*," Springer said. He pointed back down the trail. "*Banditos.*"

The man looked to where Springer was pointing. Then he looked at the boy, who shrugged. "*¿Banditos?*"

Springer nodded. "*Si.*"

He turned to show the man the bloodstains on the right rear panel of his jeans. Even if Springer could have explained how he came to have the wound, he preferred to let the man draw his own conclusions. The blood proved more persuasive than Springer's Spanish, and a moment later the mule train continued on, with Springer clinging to the pack frame of the lead mule to avoid the worst of the trail dust.

The mule pulled him for at least four miles before a series of small adobe walls and buildings suggested they were at the outskirts of a town. On the trail ahead, two people stood together, kissing. As the mule train approached, the couple separated, and their features became distinguishable. It took Springer a long time to accept that he was seeing Jason Mauser and Lisa. Only when the lead mule drew even with them did Mauser, his calm blue eyes glinting ironically, take his hand off Lisa's thigh.

Doctor Ernesto Hernandez's office occupied an adobe building on the main square of the town. A young man, with a trim mustache, thick, wire-rimmed glasses, and smooth, long-fingered hands, he had indeed studied medicine north of the border, as Mauser said, and he spoke excellent Texan. Springer lay on an examination table, his jeans bunched around his ankles and his right cheek partially numbed, while Hernandez kept up a running chatter.

"A goddamned pig did this? You sure he didn't hit you with a machete? Nasty wound. I cleaned it out and shot you full of penicillin. Looks like seven, maybe eight stitches. Even so, when the anesthetic wears off, your ass is going to hurt like a son of a bitch. It's gonna be hard to walk. And you're gonna have to keep the wound clean unless you want blood poisoning."

Arms crossed under her breasts, Lisa stood at a window that looked out on the square, where Tarahumara peddlers had spread corn, oranges, avocados, woodcarvings, and hand-embroidered articles of clothing on blankets. Some of the backpackers, assisted by Mauser, were negotiating for the goods. So far, Springer and Lisa had not spoken about the kiss. Earlier, as the mule train continued along the trail, and the man and boy raised their rifles in farewell, Springer had looked at Lisa until the dust settled. Then he hobbled toward town. Lisa fell in beside him. Her voice too emphatic, she described how she got caught up in the beauty of the scenery, how she realized too late he was missing, and how she asked

Mauser to help her search. When Springer said nothing, she asked about his missing backpack. In a detached voice, Springer told her about the banditos with the machetes and their fat leader with the pistol. Lisa met his story with a skeptical smile and asked if he had at least managed to keep his money belt and passport.

He lifted his shirt to show her the nylon pouch.

"So they took your camping equipment, including our tent, but left all of your valuables?" she observed. "That was considerate of them. Aldo, why don't you admit you threw away your pack because it was too heavy to carry?"

Her presumption of weakness on his part surprised him. It amounted to an accusation, and it was a damning one, Springer knew, because as a marathon runner Lisa could accept no weakness in herself and despised it in others—especially in her men. At the start of their relationship, he found it hard to believe a woman like her could fall for a modestly paid academic. But then she'd always been more impressed by his exploits on the Flatirons above Boulder—a hobby of his since his college days, a way to unwind and gain perspective—than by his profession.

Behind them, Mauser cleared his throat. "Actually, there have been reports of a local gang in the canyon robbing unwary tourists," he said. "That's why we always travel in large groups. And their leader's supposed to be a fat old boy in an army uniform."

Lisa lifted her slender shoulders in an irritated shrug, and they walked the rest of the distance to town in silence. After introducing them to Doctor Hernandez, Mauser went off to find the rest of the hiking party. Hernandez had listened to Springer's story of the shit-eating pig with only partial attention, his dark eyes lingering on Lisa's lips, the hollow of her throat, her breasts, and her long-muscled legs. Judging from Hernandez's frequent pauses while cleaning and stitching the wound, Springer suspected the doctor's attention continued to waver during the operation. And in spite of the partial anesthesia, every stitch brought Springer intense, drawn-out pain. But lying there on his belly, with his jeans around his ankles and Lisa standing nearby, he refused to complain. Hernandez talked nonstop, meanwhile, about life in the canyon bottom.

"I been stuck in this one-hole shithouse for two years now, and I got two more to go before my medical service is done," Hernandez said. "Then I'm going to set up shop someplace with all the amenities—women, good food, cold beer, hot showers, cable TV, more women. Y'all try living down here where the single women are all under eighteen, shy as shit, escorted everywhere by duennas, and guarded by fathers and brothers with machetes. Only one who ever gets any tail around here is Mauser, and he imports it."

At this last remark, Lisa stiffened and looked at Hernandez. Then her eyes, dark and defiant, met Springer's for an instant before she turned away.

"So Mauser gets a lot of women?" Springer asked.

"Every time he comes down here, he finds a hot little number to share his sleeping bag, lucky bastard. He ain't the brightest man I ever met, or the best looking, but he has a way with the ladies. They like the rugged, Outward Bound-instructor bullshit, so he lays it on thick. Well, you can pull up your pants, Aldo. You're all stitched up."

The door closed as Springer fastened his belt. In pesos, he gave Hernandez what amounted to twenty American dollars. Meanwhile, through the window, both he and Hernandez watched Lisa cross the square to stand next to Mauser.

As the sun topped the eastern rim of Copper Canyon, Springer lay shivering on the ground, rolled up in a blanket purchased from a Tarahumara peddler. As promised, his ass throbbed like a son of a bitch. Lisa slept next to him, warm in her sleeping bag, nothing showing but a tousle of blonde hair, a freckled nose, and a crescent of lips.

Springer looked at her, overcome for a moment with tenderness and affection but unsure if such emotions now had any meaning.

Last night, as the other backpackers went off to their tents, Lisa sat near the campfire, talking with Mauser about the run he had arranged for her—along a trail leading from the canyon bottom to a village on the rim, guided by two of Mauser's Tarahumara *compañeros*. She would take part in a traditional game in which the runners kicked a small wooden ball back and forth.

"When they're playing for real," Mauser said, "they don't stop running till the rocks wear the ball, which starts out the size of a grapefruit, to a walnut. But that takes a hundred miles or more. You'll be doing something closer to a marathon. They'll take you up one trail to their village and guide you down another to tomorrow's campsite, where we'll be waiting. It also happens to be the place where my partners have stashed the food supplies for the rest of the trip."

The plan, Lisa informed Springer, was for him to carry her pack. "That is," she added, "if you can keep from being robbed."

Springer sat near the fire, his body tilted to rest all his weight on his left cheek. "Yes, if necessary I'll fight to the death to protect your dirty underwear."

Lisa's laughter carried a bitter edge. "Sure you will. And don't eat any of my power bars," she added. "There's only enough food in my pack for one person."

This time Mauser laughed too. He and Lisa faced each other, their shoulders turned as if to fence Springer out. Lisa revealed an acute physical awareness of Mauser in the way she leaned forward, tilted her head at the same angle as his, nodded and smiled when he spoke. Such attention made a man feel special, Springer knew, having basked in it himself. He also knew he was not welcome at the fire, but he sat there, his ass and his heart aching, until the embers turned to ash.

With a tone of regret, Lisa finally said, "Well, I'd better get some rest while I can."

When she crawled into her sleeping bag, and Springer rolled up in his blanket, he said, "Lisa, you know I love you, but if you want out of our engagement, say so."

Lisa was silent for a long time. Then she said, "Don't be an idiot, Aldo."

A short time later, she snored softly. He had lain awake and stared at the stars—bright and distinct in the black sky—for a long time, trying to decide what her reply meant. Even now, as the camp woke up around them and hissing Primus stoves boiled water for coffee and oatmeal, Springer could not feel sure if she'd been telling him she still loved him or that she had, by turning to Mauser, already tacitly ended their engagement.

Lisa's sleeping bag shook and she emerged fully dressed for a marathon in a running bra, spandex shorts, and Reeboks. A commotion announced the arrival of the Tarahumara guides. Surrounded by gawking backpackers, the guides stood at the edge of the campsite, beside Mauser, and waited for Lisa to eat a power bar and drink a quart of Gatorade. Thin to the point of leathery emaciation, and no more than five feet tall, the guides had darkly tanned faces and long, black hair, tied back with white strips of cloth. They wore cotton pantaloons, peasant blouses, and tire-tread sandals. From leather thongs around their necks dangled medicine bags. The skin of their feet, cracked and callused, looked like relief maps of the canyon.

Springer, who had slept in his clothes, rolled up his blanket and stuffed it into Lisa's pack while she stretched. When she was warmed up and ready to run, he said, "Be careful, okay?"

Already in marathoner mode, Lisa gave a brief nod, her brown eyes as cool and distant as the canyon rim. A moment later, she and the Tarahumaras dogtrotted through the campsite, striking out on a trail that led to a village fifteen miles to the south, perched on a plateau a vertical mile above the campsite. As they ran, they passed their wooden ball, soccer style, to one another. Watching them pick their way around boulders and climb a series of switchbacks on a steep, brush-covered slope made Springer's entire body ache.

When Lisa's graceful, efficient form vanished over the crest of the slope, he ate a quick breakfast of half a dozen tortillas purchased yesterday from a peddler in town and got ready for the day's walk.

Besides the tortillas and blanket, Springer had bought from the peddlers a goatskin water bag and a stout, elaborately carved hardwood walking stick. Stylized human and animal figures incised on the upper half of the stick gave a sure grip while, at the tapered business end, the carver had fixed a steel spike about six inches long. Part crutch, part weapon, Springer thought when he first saw it. The stick might not frighten machete-wielding banditos, but it felt solid and reassuring in his hand.

After a three-hour hike, which Springer managed by leaning heavily on his stick, Mauser stopped beside a deep, blue-green pool. "This is my favorite spot for skinny dipping," he said. "It's the last chance to wash off the trail dust, because all afternoon we'll be climbing over a ridge that separates this branch of the canyon from the main branch. So have fun."

Some of the backpackers waded in wearing their underwear, but the more daring actually stripped and dove into the pool. Afraid to expose his wound to bacteria in the river, and unwilling to risk eating Lisa's precious power bars, Springer sat on the bank and made do with the last of his tortillas—poor fare, considering the rigors of the hike. Still hungry, he found a patch of prickly pears and, using his pocketknife sliced one of the succulent leaves and cut out a cube of meat. The flavor reminded Springer of a cross between green pepper and watermelon—moist and semi-sweet. The only problem was the microscopic needles that stuck to the blade of his knife when he cut into the cactus.

The needles were now embedded in his tongue, and Springer sat beside the river, using his teeth as tweezers.

In the river, Mauser joined the naked frolickers, revealing not only his tanned, muscular body but also the red tattoo of an eagle, done in Aztec style, across the small of his back. He swam beside a smiling young woman in her twenties, a redhead with large breasts, whose boyfriend—thin, with long blond hair, a goatee, and a perpetually sullen expression—sunned on a flat river rock. The roar of whitewater below the pool muffled their conversation, but after a while, with furtive glances at her boyfriend, the redhead waded to the other side of the river and disappeared into the brush. Mauser followed her.

The boyfriend, eyes closed, still lay in the sun. Only when a high-pitched yelp rose above the sound of the rapids did he sit up for a look around. The redhead bounded out of the brush and dove into the pool. She waded to the other side and put on her clothes while her boyfriend, glaring, went over to interrogate her in intense whispers.

"Nothing happened, Josh!" the redhead shouted.

Mauser appeared a moment later, holding his tanned, muscular body in an awkward half-crouch, his face contorted in pain. He called for help, and several of the women went to him. They let him rest his weight on their shoulders as he waded across the pool.

From beneath the talons of Mauser's Aztec eagle, in the flesh of his left cheek and upper thigh, jutted several clusters of large cactus needles. The needles were two inches long and an eighth of an inch thick at the base. They looked as if they might come from a Texas horse-crippler, though Mauser did not explain how he came to sit on one. A tough-looking woman with a no-nonsense manner and dark gray hair, drawn back in a blue bandana, retrieved a pair of tweezers from her pack, planted her left hand over the Aztec eagle for leverage, and tried to extract one of the needles. Each time she pulled, Mauser screamed "shit" and cringed away.

"They're really in there," she said. "Someone else should try. Someone stronger."

The other men looked at their feet, so Springer went over. "I'll give it a shot."

Mauser's eyes widened, the ironic gleam gone. "Oh, hell no," he said as the woman passed Springer the tweezers. "Not him."

93

"Why not?" Springer asked calmly.

Everyone looked at Mauser, who could give no straight answer, Springer knew, without revealing his designs on Lisa.

"I'll be gentle."

Putting the tweezers aside, he took out his Swiss Army knife, which included among its other tools a small pair of pliers. Like a dentist pulling a tooth, Springer took a firm grip and yanked out the first needle. There was a barb on the end, like a porcupine quill. A small strip of flesh clung to the barb, dripping blood. Springer repeated the process a dozen times, reducing Mauser to a quivering, bleeding, squealing mass of pain. A few of the needles broke off below skin level and the barbed tips would not come out even when the tough-looking woman, under Springer's direction, probed with a sewing needle.

Mauser's swearing disintegrated into a desperate, pleading repetition of "Oh Jesus!" that sounded like a prayer.

"That's all we can do," Springer said. "Maybe they'll work their way out on their own."

Mauser closed his eyes and sank, face down and quivering, onto a flat rock. The tough-looking woman, Margaret, had fetched a silver hip flask of tequila from her pack. She stood over Mauser and glanced at Springer, as if for permission. When he nodded, Margaret uncorked the flask and poured.

The ridge that separated the party from the main branch of Copper Canyon would have qualified as a mountain in most parts of the world. The trail snaked up its northern slope, following the natural contours of the terrain. In some places the trail narrowed to single file and skirted the edges of cliffs—giving the backpackers heart-pounding vistas, especially when they met a goatherd driving his animals to the canyon bottom. At other points, two mule trains could have passed each other without bumping packs.

Margaret had confiscated Mauser's topographical map and now led the party toward the forested crest of the ridge. Far behind, Springer and Mauser labored up the dusty switchbacks like lame mules. Mauser moved with a stiff, cautious gait, grunting when his pack came down on the cactus needles still embedded in him. Each grunt ended with a small, scarcely audible whine, creating an almost musical rhythmic beat—bump, grunt, whine; bump, grunt, whine.

94

Mauser's beat clashed with the music Springer would ordinarily have whistled to keep his mind off his own pain. Instead, as Springer walked, images circled his head like scavenger birds: Lisa's laughter when he came stumbling from the outhouse; the pig's shit-eating grin; Mauser's cool, scornful glance; the fat bandito's faded pistol; Mauser's hand on Lisa's thigh; Lisa smiling at Mauser over the campfire; her graceful form as she followed Mauser's Tarahumara *compañeros* up the trail. The knowledge that he was losing her—and to a slick womanizing shithead like Mauser—circled with the other vultures.

Springer looked at Mauser, hobbling up the trail ahead, and tightened his grip on the walking stick. He felt an abrupt need to terminate the heart of Mauser's rhythmic beat by embedding the walking stick's six-inch steel spike just under Mauser's Aztec eagle. Limping faster, Springer narrowed the distance between them to a few yards.

As if sensing the danger, Mauser glanced back down the trail. His cool blue eyes fastened on Springer's face and widened. Mauser ran for a few steps. Then he settled into a fast hobble—bump-grunt-whine, bump-grunt-whine—and glanced back every few steps to find that Springer was matching him, hobble for hobble. They kept up this pace for perhaps half a mile, both men laboring for breath, until Mauser finally turned and held up both hands as if in surrender.

"Stop," Mauser said between breaths. "Just stop."

Springer stood within striking distance now. But the slow, limping chase up the trail, which at first intensified his rage, soon struck him as absurd, as did the notion of skewering Mauser. He felt harsh laughter boiling up but refused to let it out, unsure what might follow. He breathed hard and felt fat beads of sweat trickle down his neck.

"Listen, man," Mauser said, "I can't help it if women like me. A lot of the women who come on my trips expect to sleep with the guide, like I'm part of the service, but that's not how it is with your girlfriend."

Springer lifted his stick. "She's my fiancée, you fuck," he said. "We're getting married in September."

Mauser shrugged and looked away. "She was giving off the vibes, letting me know it was okay to make a try for her. And she's a beautiful woman, so I did. I kissed her; she kissed me back—that's it. You want me to back off, just say so. You don't have to—"

"Drive a walking stick up your ass?" Springer asked.

Mauser glanced at the metal end of the stick, and tensed as if preparing to run, but Springer felt the rage leave him. As he stood there, facing Mauser, he thought about the Saturday in October when he and Lisa met. He had led the way up a thumb-shaped outcropping known as The Maiden, whose overhanging face made it one of the more difficult technical climbs above Boulder. After a difficult pitch, he stopped under the overhang and dangled on belay to rest his arms and trace the next series of moves. He had to attack the overhang with only his hands, and sometimes only the tips of his fingers, letting his legs swing free. The rock was good, with solid holds, so the climb depended on strength and coordination. He had doubts about making it, but a few minutes later, with a surge of adrenaline, and the metronome swing of his lower body, Springer hauled himself up the underbelly of the overhang to a sloping pitch that led to the top of the boulder. From an adjoining ridge a woman said, "Nice climb!" and he saw Lisa for the first time. At the sight of her, he lost his grip, toppled over the edge of the overhang, and fell twenty feet before his climbing buddy caught him.

As the buddy lowered Springer to the base of the rock, Lisa came over to apologize for distracting him. "I'm so sorry," she said, "but the way you climb—it's beautiful."

Springer looked into her brown eyes, flecked with green and gold. "If you'd like to make it up to me, let me buy you dinner."

When she hesitated, he said, "I've already fallen for you."

Springer's buddy groaned, and so did Lisa, but she agreed to the dinner. Later, whenever she could, she came along on his expeditions—and took part in a few modest climbs. Impressed by her strength and fearlessness, Springer taught her how to rappel and tie a decent bowline. She approached climbing like she approached accounting and running marathons—with a cool, single-minded determination to succeed. From the beginning, even long after he knew he loved her, Springer couldn't bring himself to believe a woman so beautiful and strong and ambitious would love him.

Standing there, looking up at Mauser, he had to fight the urge to weep like an eight-year-old at the thought of losing her. A colder corner of his mind told him there was no controlling Lisa—and no point in trying. She either loved him enough to be faithful, or she didn't. Even so, he gave Mauser a hard look and said, "Back off." Then he lowered the point of the walking stick to the packed dirt and waved his other arm up the trail, as if to say, "After you."

Mauser frowned at the stick, then up into Springer's face, before he turned and began his slow, rhythmic hobble toward the summit. Springer stood there until he could no longer hear the bump, grunt, and whine of Mauser's passage; then he limped after him.

A turkey vulture passed over Springer before buzzing Mauser, a short distance up the trail. The vulture circled for a while, its black eyes set in a quizzical gleam, as if unable to decide which man would collapse first. Before either had the chance to do so, Lisa dogtrotted toward them down the trail, shadowed by one of the Tarahumara guides. At her approach, the vulture caught a thermal and disappeared over the ridge. Lisa and the guide stopped beside Mauser. She waved to Springer, who lifted his walking stick in reply, but she did not come down the trail to meet him.

As Springer drew close enough to get a good look at Lisa, he felt an upsurge of complex emotions that mixed fear and love and a wistful pride. Sweat stained her running bra and trail dust darkened her ankles, but otherwise she looked fresh and strong. She stood upright, and her expression gave off a relaxed, gratified glow. In her hands, she carried the wooden ball the Tarahumaras had passed between them on the trail—a keepsake. The guide stood next to her, his stony expression softening slightly whenever he looked at Lisa, who recounted the highlights of the run, focusing on the Tarahumara village, where she had dined on oranges, avocados, and goat cheese, rolled in tortillas. Mauser listened with a distracted expression, preoccupied, Springer thought, with his own pain. When Lisa finished speaking, the Tarahumara guide said something in his own tongue, accompanied by hand gestures. Mauser stared for a moment and glanced over with a half-amused expression Springer didn't like. To Lisa, he said, "Jorge says he's never known a woman like you, who can run so well. Or one so beautiful."

Lisa smiled at the guide. "Thank you," she said. To Mauser she added, "Tell him I said thank you."

The guide spoke again, for a long time, with enough Spanish that Springer could catch a few words. The ironic gleam returned to Mauser's eyes. "Jorge is counted a great man among his people, a man of wealth and wisdom," Mauser said. "He has three sons, a large house, and a good farm, with twenty goats and three horses. His wife died two years ago, and he never thought to marry again until now."

Before Mauser finished speaking, the guide took off his shirt—white, with loose sleeves—and handed it to Lisa. He stood in front of her, the muscles of his narrow, hairless chest and slender arms tensed and trembling slightly.

Lisa clutched the shirt. She glanced at Springer, as if for help, but he could think of nothing to say. "I'm sorry," she said in a tender voice. "But I've promised to marry another man." She rested a hand on Springer's forearm and gave back Jorge's shirt.

As Mauser translated, Jorge's dark eyes searched those of Springer and Lisa and then conveyed a bleak acceptance of the situation. He gave a single, dignified nod and spoke again. This time, as Mauser translated he spoke in a voice taut with suppressed laughter. "Jorge apologizes and says Aldo must be a great runner to have won such a woman as you."

"It's not funny, Jason," she said.

Mauser's face went solemn. "No?"

She turned to Springer. Drenched with sweat and bent under the weight of Lisa's backpack, Springer imagined that in Jorge's eyes—and perhaps in Lisa's—he looked nothing like the sort of man who could win her heart. A moment later Jorge, his shirt still in his hands, gave a brief nod and ran up the trail. Springer wanted to shrug off the pack and go with him, but he wasn't runner enough.

On hearing Mauser's rhythmic whine and the tale of his encounter with the horse-crippler, Lisa insisted on carrying his backpack the final half-mile to the campsite. The transfer of Mauser's pack to her shoulders, Springer realized, amounted to more than an act of compassion. It was Lisa's way of saying that, in spite of Mauser's weaknesses and character flaws, she had chosen him. Springer hobbled along behind them, moving mechanically, the trail suddenly strange and precarious under his feet. He tried to pick individual emotions out of the stew of love and embarrassment and self-pity and impotent rage and amusement and pain that left his limbs weak and his body trembling like Jorge's.

The faces of his hiking party—solemn and glowering—greeted Mauser at the campsite. Margaret, the woman with the map, stood beside some of the more outspoken members of the party, including the redhead and her boyfriend, Josh, who idly sharpened a long hunting knife.

"Where's the food cache, Jason?" Margaret asked.

"It's supposed to be here, everything from canned salmon to Top Ramen," he said. "Under a tarp behind those rocks."

"The tarp's there but nothing else. Looks like you and your people screwed up, or else someone's stolen our food."

Mauser made a show of limping to the tarp and looking under it.

Josh continued to draw his knife across the whetting stone. "Where's the nearest town?"

With his hair pulled back in a ponytail and his features stiff with anger, Josh's face had a bony definition, Springer thought, as if one could see through his sunburned skin to the sharp edges of his skull. The goatee only exaggerated this impression. Mauser looked at Josh, and the knife, for a moment before he answered. The distance was thirty miles—two to three days' hard travel, made harder by hunger.

"Why don't we all search our packs to see where we stand, food-wise," Mauser suggested. "Let's see if we can't put together a common meal tonight."

"What about tomorrow?" Margaret demanded, and a dozen voices echoed the complaint.

"If necessary, we'll live off the land. I've seen edible plants all along the trail. No one's going to starve."

"Plants," someone mocked.

There were shouts, and one backpacker demanded a refund for the trip. Josh wondered aloud why their leader wasn't worried about starving and implied Mauser was hoarding food. He waved his knife as he spoke, urging a mutiny if necessary to get the cache of beef jerky and freeze-dried entrées in Mauser's backpack. A couple of the men nodded and moved forward.

"Try to stay calm," Lisa said. "We'll be okay as long as no one panics and does something stupid."

"Easy for you to say." Josh turned to the others. "For her, thirty miles is nothing—an easy jog. And we all know she's hot for Mauser."

Lisa stepped back and brought a hand to the base of her throat. Her expression, when she turned to Springer, mixed surprise and a fragile defiance. Suddenly weary, he closed his eyes for a moment to shut out the sight of her.

"The rest of us can't walk all that way with no food," Josh said. "I say we have a look in the mother fucker's pack."

Knife in hand, he started toward Lisa, who still carried Mauser's pack. But he stopped, and reeled back, when Springer raised his walking stick and thrust the steel spike to within inches of the goatee.

"Hey, watch it with that fucking thing," Josh said. "You could hurt somebody."

There was a ringing sound as Springer tapped the knife blade with the stick. "So could you."

Josh's eyes flicked to the knife and his bony face went blank. He looked up at Springer, then at Lisa, and sheathed the blade. "I didn't mean anything. Seriously, man, I wouldn't really hurt her."

Springer lowered the walking stick and faced the others. Mauser, he noticed, had sidled to a spot a few feet behind Lisa. "Listen, I don't like Mauser any more than the rest of you, but he's right about the edible plants. I hiked all day on some tortillas and a few bites of prickly-pear cactus meat. You have to watch the needles, but it tastes good. We'll make it, with or without canned salmon and Top Ramen."

Some of the backpackers grumbled, but Josh and the redhead said no more, and the mutiny fizzled.

Instead of pooling their food, everyone went off with their friends and loved ones to cook and eat whatever they had in their packs. For Springer, who no longer had a pack—or a loved one—this meant spreading out his blanket and harvesting a few plump leaves of prickly pear, exercising special care in cleaning his knife before cutting out the meat. Lisa laid her sleeping bag beside his blanket, giving him momentary hope that things between them weren't as bad as he feared. Then she looked up at him. She smiled, but her eyes were cool and distant. "The swordplay back there was chivalrous, but no one asked you to rescue me."

Springer stopped chewing the cactus meat. "Okay, Lisa, next time someone tries to knife you, I'll let him."

"You heard him say he wasn't actually going to hurt me."

"I heard him."

For a moment, Lisa's confident gaze wavered. "Listen, Aldo, it's just . . . no one ever stood up for me like that. Or hiked, wounded, for forty miles because he thought that's what I wanted. I don't know how to feel about it—or a lot of other things."

The emptiness in his stomach rose to his chest. "Like us?"

The sounds of the other campers talking and setting up tents intruded during a long silence. "The truth is, Aldo, I need a man who knows what he wants and takes it. I don't need a martyr. Do you think I like feeling guilty, watching you limp after me on the trail when you should have said fuck this, I'm hurt, I need medical attention and a week on the beach? Instead, you put my desires first. It's almost like you have no needs or desires of your own, so you have to hitch a ride on mine, and it's too much pressure. I want someone who can tell me, when I'm wrong, to fuck off."

Lisa gathered her belongings. Then she crossed the campsite and dropped her backpack and sleeping bag beside Mauser's tent.

At the edge of camp, near a dense clump of brush, Springer was using his walking stick to knock another helping of prickly pear leaves from their stems when, with a harsh grunt, a javelina came out of the brush and charged him. Out of reflex, Springer lifted the walking stick, and the javelina impaled itself, the force of its charge embedding the steel spike deep within its chest.

There was a rasping squeal, echoed by the cries of the backpackers, including Lisa and Mauser, who watched the struggle from across the campsite. To keep from being bitten or gored by the sharp upper tusks, Springer clung for several moments to the stick as the hog-like creature thrashed wildly, appearing to try at once to free itself and get at him. Then, heart thudding, Springer felt something give beneath his hands.

The javelina stopped struggling and flopped over, its breathing ragged.

"Oh my God," someone said.

Springer stared down at the creature, whose dark blood was draining through its nostrils and the wound in its chest. Then he looked up to see the whole camp gathered nearby, regarding him with eyes as round and surprised as an infant's.

Lisa stood next to Mauser, holding his hand and looking down at Springer's victim with an expression of horror and pity. "What the hell have you done, Aldo?"

The question sounded like an accusation of murder. "I was gathering some cactus when it charged out of the brush," he explained.

"Javelinas eat prickly pear, too," Mauser said. "Chances are, it was only defending its food supply."

Springer knew he should feel guilty, and to a certain extent he did, but as he looked at the dying light in the javelina's eyes, he realized that, beyond the initial horror at what he'd done, he felt a sense of relief. And there was something else—he was salivating.

Apparently, Margaret was having a similar reaction.

"Are javelinas edible?"

Lisa looked at the older woman. "You're not seriously considering eating this poor thing."

"We needed food, and here it is," she said. "Like the answer to a prayer."

Some of the backpackers went off to gather firewood. Over Lisa's objections, Mauser offered his outdoorsman's expertise to direct the efforts of Josh, who volunteered to serve as butcher. Years ago, Mauser said, an old Tarahumara had told him about a musk gland on the javelina's hindquarters that would, unless carefully removed, rupture and spoil the meat. Working on a plastic tarp, and following Mauser's meticulous directions, Josh skinned and dressed the carcass.

After several minutes of carving and chopping, Josh removed one of the haunches and passed it to Margaret. She turned to Springer. "As the hunter, you get the choice cut," she said.

He accepted the trophy. "This must weigh ten pounds. It's enough to share."

Lisa gave him a look of disgust and walked away. Except Josh, Mauser, and Margaret, who continued their work on the carcass, everyone else followed Springer to the cook fire, which by now was blazing at the center of camp. Using whatever utensils they had—Springer used the business end of his walking stick as a spit—the backpackers boiled, fried, or roasted strips of javelina, and a strange but savory smell filled the air around the camp. Before long, they were tearing into the meat and wiping the grease from their faces with their hands, grunting and moaning in satisfaction. The campsite looked like a scene from some throwback, pre-Columbian time of hunting, gathering, and gorging. As the hunter, Springer basked in the gratitude of the others, most of whom—without his kill—would have gone hungry.

Later, having eaten her fill, Margaret sat a little apart from the others, examining Mauser's topographical map of their route by the firelight. Springer went over and asked to have a look. With a red marker pen, Mauser had traced a path that followed the main branch of the canyon, along the Rio Cobre past a town called Urique. On the canyon rim above the town was a railroad terminal. Springer borrowed a pen and a piece of paper from Margaret and copied the route to the town, taking care to jot down what looked like important landmarks and forks in the trail.

"Are you leaving us?" Margaret asked.

He thought for a while. "Maybe."

After dark, Springer stood near the entrance to Mauser's tent. Lisa's soft, familiar laughter rose above a whispered conversation. Springer knocked on the nylon fly. "Can we talk, Lisa?"

She unzipped the fly far enough to thrust out her head without showing her body. In the reflected light of the cook fire, he made out the features of her face.

"I'll be heading out before dawn."

"What do you mean heading out? To go where?"

"Home."

Laughing, she said, "It's a long walk to Boulder, Aldo."

"I'll take the train from Urique." He hesitated and felt his heartbeat accelerate. "You're welcome to come along."

"You don't know this country. You'll only lose your way—and what's left of your valuables."

"Goodbye," Springer said and started away.

"Wait." She unzipped the fly and stepped out of the tent, wearing a T-shirt and panties. "I'm with Jason now, but that doesn't mean I want to see you hurt. Let's talk in the morning. Meanwhile, don't do anything stupid, all right?"

He started away again, then stopped. "Lisa?"

"Yes, Aldo?"

"Fuck off."

The distance to Urique, according to Mauser's map, was roughly the length of a marathon. Springer spent some restless hours rolling in his blanket. A little after midnight, the moon rose above the canyon rim, lighting the campsite and making sleep impossible. Springer's stitches itched, but otherwise he felt better than he had in days, ready for the long walk.

While the camp slept, he rolled up his blanket and gathered his belongings—his money belt, his goatskin bag of purified water, his rudimentary map, his walking stick. Navigating by moonlight, he started down the trail. The cool air smelled of sage and the pines along the canyon rim. Something large rustled in the brush—a javelina looking for revenge? Lisa might be right, he thought. In the next few hours he might take the wrong fork and get hopelessly lost, walk off a cliff, step on a bushmaster, or fall prey to the random jaguar or armed fat man. But if he made it, he thought he'd go home along the scenic route, by way of Mazatlan or Acapulco— someplace with all the amenities and no pigs. After what he'd been through, he could use a week on the beach.

The Bright Side

The woman—dark-haired, in jeans and a flannel shirt—was sitting with three unshaven men who looked like laid-off mill workers. A rip above her breast pocket offered a glimpse of creamy skin. There was something heartbreaking in the way she gripped the hand of one of the men, her brown eyes warming whenever he glanced at her. She drank a beer and smoked a cigarette with earthy relish, laughing now at what her man said. Hoback fell in love with her. Or rather he fell in love with the idea of her, for in that instant she ceased being a woman and became a metaphor.

For half an hour, he wrote nonstop, giving his latest character a name (Arlene) and a history (filled with disappointment).

The waitress, an aspiring novelist, knew not to disturb Hoback in the fever of inspiration. As always, she refilled his cup and slipped his check under the saltshaker. A moment later, when a human form intruded on his thoughts, Hoback glanced up irritably to find a man staring down at him. A black beard and the brim of a floppy hat hid most of the man's face, framing the eyes, hard and gleaming. They were pale gray and vaguely lupine, like the eyes of a sled dog.

"I'll take that," the man said and snatched Hoback's notebook from the table.

Hoback started up, but the man shoved him back into the chair with impressive ease. He ripped out the half dozen sheets of yellow legal paper containing Hoback's notes on Arlene and folded them into the zippered breast pocket of his heavy canvas shirt. Placing both hands on the table, the man brought his face to within a few inches of Hoback's. "She's mine!"

With the impact of the man's aggression came a breathy wave of onion and alcohol. Hoback drew back. Then, angry with himself, he gathered nerve enough to look into the sled dog eyes. "I don't know what your problem is, mister, but I want my notes back—now."

"A plagiarist ain't no better than a poacher," the man said. He tapped the hilt of a knife hanging from his beaded belt. "Up north I had to gut a son of a bitch who stole from my traps. I find you near one of my characters again, I'll give you the same treatment."

The man punctuated *treatment* with two painful finger jabs to

Hoback's breastbone. Then he turned and walked out of the Shack, taking Arlene with him.

"If you sit calmly, maybe you can reconstruct her from memory," Karen suggested and patted the sofa beside her.

A Careflite nurse who rescued lost hikers in the Selway-Bitterroot Wilderness, Karen knew how to stay cool in a crisis. Hoback understood this. And he admired her for it. Sometimes, though, he felt the need not for composure but for a show of sympathetic panic.

"At least this person didn't attack you physically. Maybe we should look at the bright side and be thankful you're all right."

"Maybe we should just skip the bright-side shit," he said.

She yawned, looking good despite having worked the night shift. A member of the rowing team in college, and a tireless Nordic skier, Karen stretched with the power and pleasure of a bobcat, showing a ripple of muscle in the "V" of her nightgown.

"I won't fight with you today, Peter. This man stole an under-developed character who probably wouldn't have made much of a story anyway. I'm sure your career will survive the blow."

"The son of a bitch threatened to kill me if he catches me around the Shack again."

"Then don't go back."

"It's my favorite place to write."

"Find another—like that Indian friend of yours."

"Yellowrobe?"

"He sits there for hours under the bridge and writes plays, doesn't he?" she asked. "Why can't you do that?"

"Don't you understand? That's where Yellowrobe's learned to concentrate, to do his best work. I can go to the Sixth Street Bar, and one or two other places, but I do my best work at the Shack. And if I'm ever going to crack the inner circle. . . ."

To Hoback, Missoula's literary world formed a target: the outer circle of the many wanna-bes, the middle of the minor published writers, who hoped someday to move closer to the center, and the inner of the four or five major figures (Welch, Ford, Crumley, Smith), the literary lions, with William Kittredge perched like a shining Buddha at the bull's eye.

A collection of stories published by a Seattle house put Hoback at the inside edge of the middle circle. Though not a writer of note, he was harder to dismiss than those unpublished embarrassments to the creative writing program who at dinner parties sat in the outer circle, balancing their plates on their knees. Like a shadow of Hemingway (drinking coffee, not scotch), he sat in the Shack each morning for more than a year and scribbled tales about the inhabitants of the bars and cafes of downtown Missoula—the bums, the loggers, the smoke jumpers, the cross dressers. Finally, almost broke, he'd sent the stories to a literary agent in San Jose. She warned against getting his hopes up (her other clients wrote computer manuals), but in the end she sold the collection to the Seattle house. Much encouraged, she now hoped to ride the Montana Mystique, via Hoback, straight to the New York market. And for that to happen, he needed the Shack.

Karen was frowning now. "You're not going back there, are you? So soon after this person told you to stay away?"

"What else can I do?"

She reached up and pulled him down, as always faintly surprising him with the power of her upper body and the contrasting gentleness of her lips. Later, she said, "Promise me you'll find a nice, safe place to work. Hike a few miles up the Rattlesnake, or climb Mount Jumbo, but don't go to the Shack, okay?"

For two days, Hoback leaned against a pine on the western slope of Mount Jumbo. He spent most of the time dozing in the sun, feeling cowardly and aphasic. When he started writing about a homeless person, Zeke, based on a squirrel that kept begging for food, he decided to risk a return to the Shack.

First, though, he wanted to have a talk with a friend of his, Dave, a poet who tended the Sixth Street Bar and who knew something about everyone in western Montana. At the description of the man with the sled dog eyes and the floppy hat, Dave nodded, jiggling his substantial jowls. "Yes, yes, I know who you mean. Wayne Gant. Wore grunge before it was stylish. Went to school here in town but never graduated. Got into some trouble, I think, but I never heard the details. The parents shipped him to an uncle in Alaska. I hear he killed a man up there, or that's what he claims. Came back a little over a year ago dressed like Jim Bridger. Made the mistake of pissing off Paul a few weeks back."

A biker and personal essayist, Paul worked evenings as a bouncer at the Sixth Street Bar.

"What happened?"

"Paul's shift starts soon," Dave said warily. "Maybe you should ask him."

A few minutes later, Paul entered, all leather and faded denim. Tall and blond, he had a receding hairline and a calm, sullen stare that, most nights, kept customers acting their best. With meticulous care he rolled a cigarette while listening to the story of Gant's abduction of Arlene. Finally, he asked, "Why didn't you deck him?"

Hoback could not quite meet the sullen blue eyes.

"Gant ever tried to steal my notes," Paul added, "he'd be shitting teeth for a week."

Hoback winced. "Nice image."

Paul squinted and lit his cigarette. "Says he killed some poor bastard in Alaska, huh? Not likely, unless he stabbed him in the back. I swatted him once. Right away, his eyes started to leak. He begged me to stop, saying he's got a nervous condition, can't stop himself from crying when he gets hit. Take my advice, Hoback. He messes with you again, you deck him."

From his corner table, Hoback took notes on a man who stood at the bar and gazed at a single shot long enough to anger the bartender. Judging from the tweed sport coat that stretched across heavy sloping shoulders, Hoback pegged the man as faculty for one of the university's leaner departments—history or philosophy, maybe. Framed by creases, his mouth drew down at the corners. His drooping eyes took on a distant, bewildered look as he peered into the shot glass, seeing in it something more than Jack Daniel's. Then he glanced up at the mirror, toasted his reflection, and downed the shot.

Writing nonstop, Hoback gave his character a name (Claude) and a history (fraught with loneliness and disillusionment).

He was groping toward a story line when the worn floorboards near his table creaked. He glanced up, but not in time to save his notes. Gant tore them from the notebook, folded them into his pocket, and stood looking down at Hoback, eyes gleaming.

Hoback stared at his coffee cup until Gant went away. Breathing deeply, he looked around the cafe in search of a new character. A few tables away, a woman in ranch clothes sat up straight as a gatepost in her chair, her square jaw thrust out as she told a friend, "Hank came into this marriage with a trash bag full of clothes and, by God, that's just how he'll leave it."

The friend said something Hoback missed. The ranch woman's thin lips turned up slightly at the corners. "You got that right," she said. The two of them clinked beer mugs and laughed out loud.

Hoback jotted down the trash bag line. Suddenly the notebook slipped from his fingers, he heard paper tearing, and he looked up to see Gant heading for the back room.

He and Karen had agreed he should avoid a fight even if Gant was not the murderous trapper he claimed to be. It all sounded sensible last night, Hoback thought. Now it sounded like bullshit. Standing, he followed Gant into the back room, spun him around, and threw a short, straight punch into the thickest part of the beard.

The breakfast crowd stopped eating to watch. Hoback rubbed his knuckles. Gant lay sobbing at Hoback's feet, his pale gray eyes reddened and dripping tears.

With a trembling hand, Hoback offered Gant a napkin. "Wipe your eyes," he said. "I want my notes. And the ones you stole the other day."

Blindly reaching into a pocket, Gant pulled out a wad of folded paper, which he handed to Hoback.

"I'm going to sit and write for the rest of the morning," Hoback said. "And I'll be back every day about the same time. You're free to come and go as you please, Gant, but don't bother me again."

Back at his table, Hoback found the notes on Claude and Arlene, set out in his precise, looping script. Then he came across a number of sheets covered on both sides by a random scrawl that at first appeared illegible. Squinting, he made out individual words, then sentences and paragraphs. He read it all, straight through, and then slumped in his chair, slack and breathless. When he could stand, he went over to Gant, sitting alone at a table for two, still dabbing at tears with the napkin.

"Can I sit down?" Hoback asked. "I think we should talk."

Missoula's literary elite had assembled in a grassy meadow beside a ranch-style home a few miles from Missoula for a meal of brisket and prose. A boulder served as a stage for the readers. The inner circle had formed near a keg of beer to trade quips about agents and movie deals. Denim clad members of the middle circle huddled in imitation a few feet away, straining to hear every word. The outer circle ate beef and beans and gazed—eyes round and reverent—at this gathering of the chosen.

The first reader mounted the boulder. In floppy hat, canvas work shirt, buckskin pants, and moccasins, he greeted his audience with a wild, unwavering stare.

Then he read a story as raw and strange and sensitive as he was—about a troubled young woman named Arlene.

"He's a crazy bastard," Hoback whispered to Karen, "but he can write."

They sat beyond the outer circle, balancing their plates on their knees. Karen leaned closer. "At least you can say you discovered him."

Gant finished reading. The reaction to his story started near the keg and rippled outward. The inner circle applauded; the middle circle shifted and stirred, making room for one more; along the outer circle, plates dropped and clattered to the ground; still farther out, Hoback took a look at the bright side and thought seriously about becoming Montana's first literary agent.

Swimmer

In the small, backyard pool two dozen men and women, each weighing over three hundred pounds, frolicked in the cool water like walruses.

The *Daily News* columnist, Chip Upchurch, stood on the flooded deck and gazed down at the swimmers with a slack-jawed smile, as if unable to absorb the spectacle. From a nearby deck chair, Angie Pickett watched the celebrated columnist, unsure what she detested most—this smile of awe or the cynical smirk that each week appeared in the mug shot next to Upchurch's column.

Angie went over to offer him a beer. Though one of the leaner women at the party, she still made two of him. "Mr. Upchurch, I'm glad you could come. Our association read your column about our last swim party with great interest."

Upchurch twisted off the bottle top and took a drink. Then he flashed the smirk. "I was afraid you wouldn't like it."

"Not at all," Angie lied. "Fat people are used to tolerating humor at our expense. We're grateful for the publicity. The membership of the Dallas Chapter of the Texas Organization to Aid Fat Americans nearly doubled after your column came out."

Upchurch put the beer in the crook of his arm and jotted in his reporter's pad.

"Did you bring your swimsuit this time, like you promised?"

With another glance at the crowded pool, Upchurch said, "Why don't we just sit here on the deck for a while."

Angie shrugged and returned to the chair, which creaked and threatened to give way under her weight. Upchurch dropped his reporter's pad onto a nearby table and took the chair next to Angie's.

From farther away, minus the smirk, Upchurch could have passed for a TV broadcaster—lean, dark-haired, with clearly defined features. Up close, the flaws showed—the dandruff in his slicked-back brown hair, the faded acne scars, the triangles of dark stubble his razor had missed, the old coffee stain on his blue button-down shirt that his tie didn't quite cover.

Upchurch glanced at a young man who sat on the deck and dangled his feet in the water. "He doesn't look like a member of the club, unless he's one of those thin guys that gets turned on by fat women. What do you call them? Fat admirers?"

Angie took in a deep breath of the hot Texas air. "That's my brother Jim. He's nice enough to let us use his pool."

"Oh, I see."

From the diving board a man who must have weighed a quarter of a ton yelled, "Look out below!"

The other swimmers paddled out of the way as the board bent till it touched the water. The man hit the surface halfway through a swan dive with a belly smack that sent a wave over the edge of the pool. The wave flowed over Angie's bare feet and Upchurch's leather loafers before flooding the crepe myrtles that surrounded the deck.

Upchurch took a small tape recorder from his shirt pocket and put it to his mouth. "It's astounding how awkward they are on land and how graceful they are in the water. Fat floats, I suppose, and forms a sort of internal air mattress. And their rounded edges must make it easier to glide through water. The variety among them is interesting. Some are pear shaped, with large hams and legs and smaller upper bodies. Others are well-proportioned, the excess weight evenly distributed. Still others are round and bloated, their legs bigger around than the average person's waist, the men having breasts of a size many women would envy."

The speech sounded like Darwin commenting on some newly discovered species. Angie wasn't sure whether to laugh or fume.

Then Upchurch turned to study the picnic table on a patch of lawn beyond the deck. "And look at the spread they've put together. Potato salad, barbecued sausage, lamb chops, brownies, chocolate chip bars, Rice Crispy treats, banana pudding, bean salad, coconut cake, key lime pie—all sitting next to gallons of diet soft drinks. Looks fattening as hell. They like to eat. All those myths about fat people being the product of genetics, it's just a lot of talk, isn't it? If I ate like that, I'd be as big as they are. The whole purpose of this organization is to help people accept that being fat is all right. Is that healthy? I mean, isn't it just living in denial, making it seem okay to deviate from a healthy and normal size?"

"I guess it's no worse than pretending it's okay to be a prick," Angie said.

The hand holding the tape recorder dropped onto Upchurch's lap. "So despite what you said earlier, you didn't much like my column, did you?"

She shifted the lawn chair to face Upchurch. "Half a million people read your column every week. You could help the public understand more about us, learn to appreciate what fat people suffer. Instead, like everyone else, you take a lot of cheap shots at us."

"Three quarters of a million people read my column every week," Upchurch said. "And the mail I received about that particular column was all favorable."

A quick nod left the flesh of Angie's face jiggling. "Everyone loves to make fun of us. We're easy targets, and thin people get to feel so superior."

For a while, they watched the swimmers. Overhead, on a tree limb a few feet away, there dangled a bug zapper whose violet light lured in and fried mosquitoes. The buzz and tiny flashes of light caught Upchurch's attention. He put his tape recorder to his mouth again. "This massing of flesh seems to have drawn every mosquito in North Texas. I imagine they see the members of the Texas Organization to Aid Fat Americans the way the members see their potluck dinner—banquet time."

One of the TOAFA members, Mindy Moorehead, came over then to offer Upchurch another beer. "Here you go," Mindy said in a husky voice.

"Uh, thanks," Upchurch muttered.

"No problem, Chippy."

Mindy had dark hair, well styled, and a pretty, wholesome-looking face that, Angie thought, might have been beautiful if she were a hundred pounds lighter. She struck a pose before Upchurch, her breasts uplifted, one hip thrust to the side, and lit a cigarette, which she pulled on with such force that even in the afternoon sun the end glowed red. As she exhaled smoke, she winked down at Upchurch and strutted back toward the pool. The other swimmers whooped or whistled.

Angie's wide face drew down in disapproval. "You enormous sleaze."

Mindy stopped and glanced back at Upchurch. "Is he man enough for this much woman? I don't think so." As the others laughed, Mindy added, "I'd take you on anyhow, honey, but a skinny little boy like you, I'd likely bust you in two—snap your back like a winter twig."

Upchurch gave Mindy a blank, slack-jawed stare.

"She's one of your well-proportioned specimens," Angie observed. "Models clothes for the big and tall women's catalogs. Might make a good interview subject."

Upchurch nodded slowly. "I suppose so."

"Just don't let her get you alone. She won't take no for an answer."

"What?" Upchurch looked at Angie. "You're suggesting that woman would try to assault me sexually?"

"Not assault, but she's very persuasive," Angie said. "Don't worry, though. You'll be fine as long as you stay out here by the pool."

The swimmers were playing Marco Polo. The splashes, shouts, and laughter made it hard to talk, but Angie caught Upchurch watching Mindy, looking down whenever Mindy turned her dark eyes his way.

The game ended when one of the TOAFA members announced he wanted to read the group his latest poem. The poet, Daniel, was what Upchurch had earlier referred to as a fat admirer. A thin man, with a thinner mustache, he took to the stage—the diving board. As Daniel read with a slight lisp, Upchurch switched on his tape recorder. Titled "Wanted," the poem went like this:

> Wanted: Real woman,
> with beautiful, full moon face.
> Wanted: woman with bountiful rolls and folds of fat,
> smooth wide buttocks and enormous breasts, fertile and
> rich as the earth.
> Wanted: Real woman,
> Rubenesque and sensuous.
> Wanted: woman who jiggles when she laughs and laughs
> when she jiggles.
> Wanted: Real woman.

"Uh, that's the end," Daniel said. The swimmers applauded, and two Rubenesque women went over to give the poet rich and fertile hugs.

Upchurch clicked off his tape recorder. "Do you have anything to drink around this place besides beer—something stronger?"

Angie pointed to the banquet table. "There's vodka on the table over there, behind the bag of Ruffles."

Large red plastic drink cups were stacked up near the soft drinks. Upchurch took one, scooped up ice from a cooler, and filled the cup with vodka. As he poured, Mindy went over to stand beside him. She touched his arm, leaned close, and spoke to him. They talked for a while, and the color of Upchurch's face gradually deepened. Then he shook his head. Mindy shrugged and returned to her lounge chair at the opposite end of the deck. When Upchurch came back, he took long gulps of the vodka. His blue button-down was now dark with sweat.

"Tell me about yourself," he said. "What was it like growing up? I mean, were you always heavy?"

A bottle of sunscreen made flatulent noises as Angie squeezed lotion onto her hand. The lotion smelled like coconut and lime. As she spread it on her arms and legs, she said, "I don't think I'd like to be the subject of another of your columns, thank you."

Upchurch raised his free hand as if swearing an oath. "I just want some background information, the kind of details I'll need in order to ask intelligent questions. I won't take notes or record the conversation, all right? And I promise not to quote you."

Angie held the bottle of sunscreen like a weapon, aiming it at Upchurch's face. "You want to know how the other kids teased me from age seven on? How I came home from school crying every day? How I tried Teen Tops and Weight Watchers and Cambridge and every other diet and none of them worked? How I'm smart as hell but had to give up my dream of teaching college because I couldn't face a classroom full of thin, mean-spirited little bastards who assume I'm stupid because I'm fat?"

Upchurch gulped his vodka. "Did you have much of a social life, go out on dates, anything like that?"

Angie didn't speak for a while. Finally, she said, "I was in my twenties before a man asked me out. He was an ex-biker with a scarred right eye, but he said he loved me and I believed him. Six months later he dumped me without a goodbye. He took my camera, my laptop, and my credit cards, and he cleaned out my bank account. Ask any of the men and women here, and you'll get a similar story. That's why this organization is so important to us. That's why we keep hoping someone like you will understand us, and help us reach out to other people with the same problem."

With no trace of the smirk, Upchurch said, "I do want to understand." Then it was confession time. "Listen, Angie, my mother was big. Bigger than you. When I was young, before elementary school, I didn't think of her as fat. I used to love how soft and warm she was, and how I'd disappear in her whenever she hugged me. When I started school, the other kids laughed when they saw her. They made fun of her, called her names, teased me. I started hating that she couldn't control herself—just stop eating. Sometimes she'd sit down in a restaurant, and the chair would break, and everyone in the place would look at us and laugh as I tried to help her up. To the people at school and in the neighborhood, I was always the fat woman's son. She humiliated me, and, God forgive me, I hated her for it. After I went away to college, I never looked back. I haven't seen her for years."

Angie stared at him.

"I know," Upchurch said. "I'm a prick. If it helps, I hate myself for it."

She glanced away. "It doesn't help."

Another woman, Barbara something, came up then, her chin held down, her eyes fixed on the wet concrete of the deck. At nearly five hundred pounds, Barbara was by far the largest woman in the organization. Her swimsuit consisted of an enormous pair of black shorts and a black T-shirt—both stretched thin. She muttered something Angie couldn't quite make out.

"Excuse me?" Angie said.

The woman still looked at the deck. "The bathroom," she said. "Where's the bathroom?"

Angie gave her directions and watched as Barbara trudged toward the house. Then she turned and found Upchurch staring at her.

"You feel it too," Upchurch said. "I saw the disgust on your face."

For a while, Angie checked the set of her facial muscles and tried to fit her expression to her feelings and her feelings to words. Then she shrugged. "I can't stand that she's so humble she won't look anyone in the eye. She should have some pride. I feel sorry for her, but as long as she's too shy to be comfortable asking directions to the bathroom, I'll also feel a measure of contempt."

Upchurch drained his glass and went for a refill. He quickly drank it down. "Maybe I'll take a dip after all," he said. "Where can I change clothes?"

Angie pointed to the guestroom over the garage where the other swimmers had changed into their suits. As Upchurch climbed the outside staircase, Mindy got up from her recliner and followed him.

The splashes and laughter died as Mindy entered the guestroom and shut the door behind her. A short time later, there was a muffled cry, but whether uttered in pain or pleasure, or by male or female, Angie couldn't tell. Then other sounds—moans and violent thumps and thrashes —reached the deck. Angie glanced at the guestroom door. Having once witnessed one of Mindy's seductions, she had a clear mental image of the conflict—of Upchurch, outmatched, resisting for as long as he could, of Mindy using force until force no longer became necessary, of the two of them performing a series of contortions to compensate for the size difference, and ease the strain on Upchurch's spine, of the seduction process beginning again.

Angie's brother Jim came over to sit in Upchurch's chair, interrupting these thoughts. "Well, did you manage to change the bastard's mind about your group?"

Upchurch's pocket tape recorder rested on a table. Angie rewound the tape, stopping at times to listen. When she pressed play, Upchurch's voice described the categories and feeding habits of the obese. As they listened to the speech, Angie recalled another swimming pool, years ago, where the family stopped during a trip to the Rockies. She was twelve at the time, and already heavy. As she approached the water, a boy Jim's age shouted, "Here comes Godzilla." The remark snatched away all her anticipated joy at cooling off in the pool, and she merely stood at the side, too frozen with humiliation to cry. Jim waited until no one was looking; then he swam over and punched the boy.

As the tape reached the end of Upchurch's Darwinian commentary, Angie pressed record. "The fat admirer undergoes three stages of development: discovery, denial, and acceptance," she said. "Congratulations, Chip, you've achieved all three stages in a single afternoon."

Above the garage, the sounds of lovemaking reached a crescendo and gradually died away. The chair creaked as Angie got up. "Time for dinner," she announced and ushered people toward the food. "I won't have everyone staring at them when they come down. At least we can be busy doing what we do best."

When Upchurch descended the stairs, he bent his stiffened joints like someone much older. He held his clothes in a bundle under one arm, his shoes in the opposite hand. His bony frame was bare except for a baggy pair of maroon swimming trunks.

As Upchurch passed Angie's chair, he dropped his clothes and shoes onto the wet deck. "I think I'll take a dip," he said.

He flung himself in and floated face down for a long time. Finally, he paddled slowly toward the deep end. As he swam, he looked like a sea otter—dark hair slicked back, nose just above the surface. After a couple of laps, he slowly pulled himself from the pool.

"I have to go," he said.

"In your swimsuit?" Angie asked. "Don't you want to change back into your street clothes?"

Upchurch looked at the bundle of clothes on the deck, then up at the guestroom where Mindy still waited. "No."

"We're having another party in August," Angie said. "You're welcome to come."

Upchurch gathered his clothes and shoes and started away, the tie dragging behind him through puddles of water.

"Wait." Angie hurried after him and wedged the tape recorder between his bare chest and the bundle of clothes. Upchurch accepted the recorder with a blank, slack-jawed stare, and Angie almost felt sorry for him. With a gentle smile, she patted him on the shoulder and said, "Call your mother."

Assassinations

In the summer of 1963, the whole neighborhood gathered on a bluff above the Interstate to watch John and Jackie Kennedy drive by in their open limousine. The Kennedys were on their way to Air Force One after attending the graduation ceremony at the Air Force Academy. Four years later, Cole still remembered Jackie's white dress and matching hat. And he remembered the color of John Kennedy's hair—tarnished copper—startling to a kid who knew the president only from black and white television images. Most of all, he remembered how Dominique Scabbone raised both her hands as if sighting down the barrel of a rifle and said, "Pow, pow, pow."

The sound of Mrs. Scabbone's hand as she slapped Dominique's face echoed the gunshots. Dominique surprised Cole when she didn't cry. She pushed her black hair out of her eyes, looked at him, and grinned.

The grin stuck in Cole's mind. Dominique was a tomboy, the only girl in his class who liked to hunt and play army, but grinning like that she looked beautiful. Cole saw the grin many times after President Kennedy died because Dominique grinned whenever she shot something. And she was grinning now as she passed through the line of stunted blue spruce that formed the back border of Cole's yard.

Dominique cradled in her arms her father's Remington, whose black barrel gleamed. Her jeans pockets bulged with extra bullets.

"Ready?" she asked.

Cole's own pockets bulged with sunflower seeds. He had no gun, only the bow and arrows he got for Christmas. Fiberglass and the color of the key lime pie, the bow looked harmless. It was a toy, almost. But on long summer afternoons, when Dominique Scabbone brought over her father's Remington repeater, Cole used the bow to hunt the rabbits and squirrels that lived in the wooded foothills near their homes. He even shot at a deer once. But unlike Dominique, who shot butterflies, snakes, salamanders, turtles, fish, birds, raccoons, and stray Weimaraners, Cole never hit anything. And though Cole often asked, Dominique would let no one touch her father's Remington.

Cole's mother always told him to stay close to home. But she would be out for hours, ringing doorbells and pushing Skin So Soft. His father, a corporate safety director, always told him to stay away from Dominique —the only kid Cole's age in the neighborhood—because she was reckless. Neither of Cole's parents knew Dominique could pick the lock on Mr. Scabbone's gun cabinet, and Cole wasn't going to tell them.

Woodman Creek ran through a shallow canyon along the interstate. Houses overlooked the creek from nearby hillsides, but Cole and Dominique, in jeans and dark T-shirts, could hunt among the willow thickets or under the sandstone bluffs without attracting attention. To the drivers of cars and trucks roaring along the Interstate above, they were invisible.

A head taller than Dominique, Cole bent at the waist, his bow held horizontal to the ground, an arrow on the string. The feathered ends of the other arrows protruded from a quiver, worn like a sword sheath on his belt. He wore his hair short, and the breeze blowing down the creek bed cooled his scalp. As he hunted, he lifted his feet high and placed each canvas shoe on sand or sandstone, avoiding leaves and twigs. For a clean shot Cole had to get close to the game—unlike Dominique, who shoved branches aside and stomped through clotted leaves.

The stomping flushed a cottontail. Dominique brought the Remington's black barrel up; a high-pitched squeal followed the shot.

Both of them ran to where the cottontail lay. One leg twitched and white bands formed at the outer edges of its eyes.

"Put it out of its misery," Cole said. "My dad says a good hunter never lets an animal suffer, even if he has to shoot it again."

"Shoot it again?" Dominique put the end of the Remington's barrel against the cottontail's twitching foot. "You mean here?"

"In the head, stupid."

Dominique put the barrel against the puff of tail. "How about here?"

This time she pulled the trigger, and the cottontail's rear legs jerked. She began firing rapidly, putting bullets everywhere but in the cottontail's head.

As shot after shot echoed from the bluffs, Cole turned away and walked downstream, once again holding his bow ready.

The tracks of skunks, raccoons, porcupines, coyotes, and something big—a bobcat or cougar—marked the wet sand. The creek drained the slopes of the Rampart Range, a few miles west of the highway, and people who lived closer to the mountains sometimes saw bears. Alone, Cole had hiked upstream as far as the ranch at the foot of the Ramparts, where a barbed-wire fence bearing No Trespassing signs dipped into the creek to keep cattle from wading under. He had stopped and gazed at the rocky, pine-covered slopes. Dominique would have ignored the signs, he thought. She would have crossed the fence and shot a cow or calf. Someday, he wanted to cross the fence and climb the mountains. And someday, he hoped, Dominique would come face to face with something big—a bobcat or cougar or bear; something that wouldn't let out a high-pitched squeal, roll over, and die. But she liked to kill better than she liked to walk, so most days they hunted close to home.

A mile downstream, the canyon flattened out and the creek emptied into a series of ponds near the South Gate of the Air Force Academy. Ducks roosted among the cattails and marsh grasses, though none showed themselves today. Only the eyes and nostrils of frogs dotted the surface of the pond.

Dominique killed three frogs before the others vanished. The dead ones' legs kicked as they bobbed on the surface. She stood on the grassy bank, the rifle ready, and fired each time a frog came up for air.

Cole sat on a rock and cracked sunflower seeds with his teeth. The worst fight he and Dominique ever had started here, at the pond, in the days before Dominique got her hands on the rifle. At the time, they were fishing for frogs—casting a spinning lure beyond a frog's head, reeling in the line with a slow, easy motion until the lure was a few inches from the target, then tugging hard.

Usually, they missed. Sometimes, they hooked the frog's head, lip, leg, back, or belly. Dominique kept their catch in a bucket. She planned to use the frogs for a basement science experiment, she said, and for the sake of science Cole didn't mind helping. But that was before he knew her well. He enjoyed the challenge of frogging until his hook lodged in the eye socket of a bullfrog, somehow encircling the eyeball without puncturing it.

For a long time, Cole worked to remove the hook without hurting the frog more, but the barb caught on the eyeball. He stood there, lightheaded, the hook in one hand and the struggling bullfrog in the other.

Dominique reached out her hand. "Give him here," she said. "I'll get the hook out."

Careful to keep slack in the line, Cole handed her the frog.

She looked at it. Then she yanked hard on the line and threw the bullfrog as far as she could into the pond.

Cole shoved her when she grinned. Dominique punched him, but Cole was heavier and stronger. He soon pinned her to the wet ground. Later, he couldn't have said why he did it, but as they struggled he leaned down and kissed Dominique on the lips.

She went slack. When he stopped kissing her, she looked up at him, her brown eyes narrow and flat. "Get off."

Cole scrambled to his feet. He was collecting his fishing gear, to go home, when she punched him in the ear. This skirmish lasted longer than the first, and he had to fight harder, but it ended the same way, with Cole sitting on her chest.

"I'm not getting up till you promise to stop fighting," he said.

And so it went, all the way home—ambushes, short, fierce struggles, broken promises. Each time, Cole had to decide whether to sit on Dominique forever or let her go. He wondered if he should knock her out, but his parents taught him never to hit a girl. By the time they fought their way to his backyard, Dominique still showed no sign of giving up, no sign of reason. For the first time, looking into her flat brown eyes, Cole felt scared. He made it to the house by shoving her down and running for the door. Even then, as he reached the porch, a rock glanced off his skull.

Cole clapped a hand to the back of his head, and it came away bloody. He fought back tears. "You bitch."

Before she moved out of sight beyond the line of stunted spruces, Dominique said, "Next time I'll kill you."

After the fight, Cole swore never to see Dominique again. But he soon tired of the long summer afternoons in the back yard, spent kicking a football or dodging the arrows he shot straight up in the air. Within a few weeks, he went back to ranging the hillsides with her, digging tunnels into the creek banks, building forts, playing army, and waging spear grass wars. He didn't try to kiss her again. And he took care to prevent arguments from becoming fights, even when Dominique did something crazy—like empty her rifle into a cottontail.

"Look at that." Dominique pointed the black barrel of the Remington at a twin-engine airplane. The airplane flew over a landing field to the north, leaving a trail of parachutes.

Cole spit out a sunflower seed husk. "Cool. Must be the Air Academy cadets."

"Must be stupid bastards to jump out of a perfectly good airplane."

"It takes guts. My dad saw a cadet die once. The parachute opened wrong and didn't even slow the guy down. Imagine falling thousands of feet, watching the ground get closer and closer, knowing you're about to die."

"Smack," Dominique said and laughed. "Cadet pancake."

Cole frowned and Dominique laughed harder. She aimed at the lead parachute. "Pow, pow, pow," she said. "How far away are they? Two miles?"

Cole shaded his eyes with his hand. "Maybe less. Why?"

She answered by pulling the trigger until the Remington was out of bullets. As she dug in her pockets for more, the parachutes dipped behind the cattails.

Cole sat there, a sunflower seed between his teeth. This wasn't like the cottontail—or the ghostly, half-crazed Weimaraner. This wasn't something Cole could turn and walk away from. He didn't know what to do, so he sat there with the sunflower seed between his teeth. Then he spit out the seed and started laughing.

"Jesus," he said. "You're crazy."

Dominique grinned down at him.

"You know those little black dots under the parachutes?" Cole said. "Those are people."

She shook her head. "Look like pigeons."

"You can't shoot at people." Cole picked up his bow. "They'll put you in jail. We have to get out of here, now, before the police come."

Bent at the waist, weapons ready, they ran upstream, moving from one clump of willows to the next. Far upstream, they stopped under a cliff to catch their breath. Dominique aimed the Remington at the sky. "Pow, pow, pow," she said and laughed so hard that she collapsed onto the sand.

This time, Cole refused even to smile. "You could've killed those guys."

Dominique went on laughing.

"Don't ever do that again."

"Shoot pigeons?"

"Promise me."

Dominique nodded. "Come on, I have an idea."

Cole glanced down the creek bed toward the pond. "Let's go home. They're probably looking for us."

She turned onto a game trail beyond the cliff and started up a steep embankment. Cole watched from the creek bed for a minute. Then he followed her.

Above Woodman Creek, the trail wound through thickets of scrub oak and into a stand of ponderosa pines. It ended at the crest of a bluff that overlooked the Interstate—the same bluff from which, four years ago, they watched John and Jackie Kennedy.

Dominique sat on a rock at the edge of the bluff. Cole stood next to her, looking down at the passing cars.

"What are we doing here?"

"You'll see."

The sandstone cliffs fell in two steps to Woodman Creek, where a four-lane steel bridge spanned the canyon. The sound of the tires rose in pitch as cars and trucks passed over the bridge. Cole stood next to Dominique and plucked his bowstring with the tip of an arrow, making a low musical sound, like an off-key guitar.

The drone of an engine drew Cole's eyes north. The plane was passing over the airfield, leaving another trail of parachutes.

Cole pointed at the parachutes and turned his head to tell Dominique they had nothing to worry about. That's when she started shooting.

There were three shots. A station wagon swerved, hit the guardrail of the bridge over Woodman Creek, skidded across two lanes of traffic, and sprayed plumes of dirt as it spun into the median strip beyond the bridge.

An orange moving van almost hit the station wagon and wobbled for a moment before recovering. The truck pulled onto the shoulder of the road, brakes hissing. Dominique grinned and adjusted her aim to follow the truck driver, who climbed from the cab and ran toward the station wagon. At the shot, the driver crouched, glanced up toward the bluff, and took cover behind his truck.

The black barrel shifted to the station wagon—a beige Country Squire with a band of fake wood paneling along the doors.

"Don't!" Cole screamed as Dominique fired again.

Tiny black dots appeared on the station wagon's hood and roof, and Cole heard the delayed thump of impact that followed each shot.

The station wagon door opened and the sound of crying children reached the bluff. A woman got out, carrying the slack body of a small child in her arms. Blood stained the front of the woman's white dress. Three other children, a boy and two girls, got out and ran with the woman to the moving van, whose driver waved to them.

Dominique thrust her hand into her jeans pocket.

Cole pulled the rifle out of her hands and stepped back, the rifle and his bow clutched in a shifting bundle against his chest.

Dominique's face was pale, her brown eyes sharp and gleaming. "That's my rifle. I don't want you touching it. I never said you could touch it."

Cole felt weak and out of focus. "You promised you wouldn't do it again."

Dominique's grin showed all her teeth, white and even. "Shoot pigeons?"

"You shot a kid."

Cole backed to the edge of the bluff and Dominique followed. He shifted the Remington into one hand and, holding it by the barrel, extended it as far as he could reach over the brink of the upper cliff. "Get back."

"If you drop it, I'll kill you."

Cole let the rifle fall. As he ran, he heard Dominique's squeal of rage, followed by the splintering of wood far below. The next thing Cole expected to hear was Dominique's feet on the trail behind him. The thought made him run faster.

At the creek bed, Cole crouched on his knees behind a clump of willows. He drew an arrow from the quiver, notched it on the bowstring, and aimed at the point where the trail met the creek. The jolt of his heart made it hard to hold the bow steady. He waited, the bowstring drawn back, the arrow bobbing with his heartbeat, for Dominique to come grinning down the embankment toward him.

Before long, Cole's arm shook so much he had to relax the bow. The image of the woman in the white dress, holding the child's body as she ran, stayed in his mind. To go home would mean climbing the hillside, climbing toward Dominique, so Cole went upstream instead.

Distant sirens were coming closer. There would be policemen at the bridge. He could ask for help, tell them what he knew, make sure Dominique didn't shoot anyone else. But he looked away when she shot the Weimaraner and laughed when she shot at the cadets, so they'd say he encouraged her. And when he took the Remington away, too late to help the kid, he must have left fingerprints on the barrel. Dominique would know that. She might even say he did the shooting.

Cole heard feet stomping through leaves. The sound came from behind him, from beyond a bend in the creek.

To avoid leaves and twigs, he lifted his feet high as he ran, careful to step only on grass or rock or sand. He passed under the bridge, far below the shouts and sirens, and reached the next bend without seeing or being seen by Dominique. The sandstone walls were high here, and too steep to climb. Less than a mile away, the creek bed was cut by a deep gully filled with rusting cars. Cole played there sometimes. The cars formed a giant staircase to a neighborhood west of the highway, where there were lots of places to hide.

From behind him, under the bridge, came the distant sound of footsteps. Cole ran on as fast and quietly as he could. The creek passed under a metal aqueduct before curving north and flowing almost straight for half a mile. Once, dared by Dominique, Cole had crossed the aqueduct like a tightrope walker, balancing with his arms thrust out, looking only at the steel pipe ahead of his feet and ignoring the long drop to Woodman Creek. It was the only time Cole could remember impressing her. And it was the only time he ever felt truly scared—until now, as Dominique came steadily after him through the rotting leaves under the bridge.

The willows in the creek bed gave only scattered cover and, out of breath before he was halfway to the rusting cars, Cole knew he had to find a good hiding place. Just ahead, the trunk of a fallen ponderosa angled into the creek from the top of a cutbank. There were deep shadows under the bank, screened by the brown needles still clinging to the tree's remaining branches.

Cole's first urge was to go straight to the cutbank. Instead, he ran upstream for a short distance, letting a handful of sunflower seeds trickle through his fingers. A few yards beyond the ponderosa, where the grass grew lush, he stepped into the creek and waded into the shadows under the cutbank. Kneeling in the cool water, he put an arrow on his bowstring.

A short time later, through the screen of brown needles, he saw Dominique. In her arms she cradled what was left of the Remington. The fall had split the stock, leaving a long, triangular sliver of wood below the trigger guard. Dominique held the sliver in her right hand, her finger on the trigger. Any hope that the rifle itself was broken ended with Cole's glimpse of Dominique's pale face and hunter's walk—eager and half-crouching.

Her flat brown eyes searched the creek bed, probing the willow thickets. She bent to pick up one of the sunflower seeds and ran for a few steps along the trail of seeds he had left her. Then she stopped and turned toward the shadows under the dead tree. Cole fought the impulse to run, to flush from cover like a frightened cottontail, but the key lime bow—almost a toy—made him different from the cottontail, from the Weimaraner, from the kid.

"I know you're there."

Cole stayed still, bent low over the water, as a bullet grazed the trunk of the tree and struck the cutbank.

"Nobody but you knows I shot anybody," Dominick said. "And nobody knows we were together. You didn't tell your mom, did you?"

She was coming closer, angling upstream toward a point where the trunk of the ponderosa would give him no cover. Aiming the bow at a steep angle, Cole shot an arrow high into the air over the creek bed. Then he fitted another arrow to the bowstring, and stood up.

Dominique's brown eyes followed the first arrow to the peak of its flight. Not until Cole released the second arrow did she look at him. The arrow hit her high in the chest. The rifle went off, and Dominique fell back onto the wet sand.

Behind the ponderosa, Cole knelt in the cool creek and cried until Dominique stopped moving, stopped making sounds. The first arrow was stuck in the grass at the other side of the creek. He put it back in his quiver.

Cole didn't want to touch the body, didn't want to look into the flat brown eyes. So he left her there, the arrow in her chest. As he reached the gully filled with junked cars, he heard shouts—deep and angry—coming from the creek bed behind him. He paused at the foot of the giant, rusted staircase, wanting to climb to the safety of his backyard, to the home that smelled of Skin So Soft. But he knew he could not go back there, that having ambushed and killed his only friend he no longer belonged. He walked up Woodman Creek toward the ranch at the foot of the Rampart Range, leaving the angry shouts behind. He would ignore the No Trespassing sign, cross the barbed-wire fence, climb the rocky, pine-covered slopes of the mountains—see what he could see before they hunted him down.

Archipelago

At the sight of her husband pouring milk of magnesia into a tall glass of Chivas, Marian Winterberg thinks she might like to kill him. The minty odor of the concoction—heavy and sweet—reaches her at the kitchen door. The odor fills the living room, emanating not so much from this particular glass as from the many glasses before it, via the pores that have grown in number as Otto's belly has grown in size—now filling the worn leather recliner to overflowing.

As Marian watches, Otto stirs the concoction with a teaspoon and presses a remote control button to advance a cartridge of slides. On reaching a photograph of a long ago trip to Hawaii, he heaves his body into an upright posture.

"Marian? Marian. Come in here and see this," Otto says. Then more softly: "Look at us. We're so young and smiling. Jesus." He sips the concoction, leaving a milk of magnesia mustache on his upper lip. "Marian?"

From the kitchen door, Marian sees the image of a slender, dark-haired young woman in a black bikini sitting on the lap of a slender, dark-haired young man. She puts a hand to her face and touches the wrinkles under her eyes, the loose flesh under her chin, the lips tight with strain.

"I swear I don't see how you can stand to sit here all day, staring at those goddamned pictures."

"Look at us. Remember this trip? Oahu, 1965? God, those were good times."

"Don't," Marian says. "I'm in no mood for one of your sentimental journeys."

Other than Otto, the living room is spotless, but Marian dusts and straightens everything: the brass lamps, the teak bookshelves and coffee tables, the framed paintings of oil rigs set in Texas landscapes, the slide projector, the bottle of Chivas. Moving to the fireplace mantle, she dusts and straightens the matched pair of Samurai swords, the cutlery sharpener, Otto's potassium pills, and the picture of Otto in his pilot's uniform, looking tidy and a lot thinner.

Otto advances to a slide that shows the fighter pilot, the young wife, and their little dark-haired daughter eating roast pig at a luau, wearing smiles and leis. In the next slide, the wife and daughter are laughing as the fighter pilot mimics the main course—an apple in his mouth, cheeks blown up, eyes bulging.

Marian looks at the slide for a long time. Then she draws the short sword from its sheath and picks up the sharpener. She sits on the sofa and begins honing the sword with a series of graceful, rhythmic movements.

"It's perfectly beautiful outside, Otto. Why did we work so hard all our lives if all you wanted to do was sit around and drink and look at musty old slides?"

Otto's teaspoon makes a rattling, ringing noise that Marian feels in the nerve endings of her fingers. She sharpens the sword until the feeling goes away, looking up only when Otto begins to snore.

"Otto? Otto. Don't you dare fall asleep when I'm talking to you."

Retrieving the bottle of pills from the mantle, Marian stands over him, sword in one hand, pills in the other. The sweet, minty odor of Chivas and milk of magnesia is stronger now, and Marian realizes that Otto has spilled his drink down the front of his pajamas. The liquid has pooled in a triangular cavity formed by the juncture of Otto's belly and chest and is spreading. "Otto, wake up and take a goddamned pill."

Otto goes on snoring, eyes half-open but sightless. His lips flap. The rolls of fat under his chin expand and contract with each breath. Marian lifts the sword over her head and wonders how many strokes it would take to decapitate him. Too many, she decides.

"Mother! What are you doing?"

Annie stands at the open door to the backyard in a yellow string bikini. Her slender, sunburned body is so bright with tanning oil Marian has to squint.

Marian lowers the sword. "Trying to wake your dad."

A moment later, Annie is beside the recliner, mixing the piña colada scent of her tanning oil with the odor of Otto's spilled drink. She looks up at the image projected on the wall.

"Oh, I always loved these slides."

Returning to the sofa, Marian hones the sword. "What could you possibly see in them? You were five years old then."

"They bring back the times when we were a family."

"What are we now? A herd?"

Annie pauses for a while, as if searching for the right word. "We're an archipelago."

Marian looks up.

"It's a body of islands," Annie says with a look of sadness. "So are we."

"Did you hear that, Otto? After all those years at Southern Methodist, our darling little daughter has become a poet. Aren't you proud?"

Otto's eyelids flutter, but he goes on snoring.

Marian points the sword at the peak of his belly. "As you can see, the big island—the continent—is as proud of his little island as I am."

Another slide comes up: Otto in a swimsuit, flexing the muscles of his arms, chest, and stomach with an expression of mock ferocity. "Look at Daddy," Annie says. "So thin, so handsome."

Marian glances instead at the portrait of Otto above the fireplace, thinking about the day they met. "When he came into the cafe, I dropped three cups of coffee and a tuna melt." She gave him the best service any man ever had and wrote her phone number on the ticket. Otto called her the same night. "I wasn't bad looking myself in those days."

"Not too bad, judging from the pictures," Annie says.

"Otto was confident, full of big dreams. In his eyes you could see he was going to be a success. And for a long time, he was."

Beneath the tanning oil, Annie's sunburned skin has sprouted goose bumps, and she's looking up at Otto's picture with a soft, fragile smile that causes Marian to tighten her grip on the sword.

"Tell me the truth," Marian says. "What could be more pathetic than a fat old wildcatter who stinks of booze and couldn't come within fifty miles of a gusher if his life depended on it?"

With a troubled frown, Annie takes the empty glass out of Otto's lap and places it on the floor next to the bottle of Chivas. "Daddy's not *fat*."

Marian laughs despite a stab of pain under her breastbone. "Oh no?"

Standing, she places the point of the sword against Otto's belly, just below the stain left by the spilled drink. Twisting her wrist, she cuts off a button already stretched tight, and the flesh surrounding Otto's navel spills out of the pajama top. "What do you bet I could shove this in up to the hilt and never strike a vital organ?"

"Stop it," Annie says in a harsh whisper.

"We might strike oil, though. That's more than Otto's been able to do for the past ten years."

In the next slide the Winterbergs are walking up a black sand beach in a loose cluster, the fighter pilot looking straight at the camera, the young wife tilting her head to look into his face, the daughter gazing at the waves breaking a short distance away.

Standing over Otto, Marian goes on sharpening the sword. "Was a decent retirement too much to ask after all the years we spent in the oil camps, hiding from creditors? Otto liked to play the high roller, never letting on that everyone from tool pushers to the IRS had a lien on the rigs. We would've lost it all, too—the house, the cars, everything—if it wasn't in my name."

"What good does it do to dredge it up again?" Annie asks.

More slides flash onto the wall, showing the Winterberg Oil Company headquarters, the drill rigs, and Otto and his crew in hard hats and coveralls, black with crude—in the heady days of gushers and serious money. "I wanted to quit, take our profits and get out of the business," she says. "Otto had other plans."

Annie looks away. "I know."

"You couldn't possibly know."

"Daddy gave the money to that Brazilian, Señor Ortiz."

At the mention of the name, Marian almost drops the sword. "Listening at our door, were you?"

"I was lying in bed, trying not to listen while you and Daddy screamed at each other."

Ortiz was mixed up in a sure thing, options on huge tracts of oil-rich land in Venezuela, but he needed a partner. The Winterbergs would net ten times their money in six months, with the IRS none the wiser. Otto gave away their future with a handshake—no lawyers, no contracts, not so much as an I.O.U. A matter of honor, Otto said, so he let Ortiz run off to Brazil with most of their fortune.

"That's when the IRS moved in and grabbed up what was left," Marian says. "Like I told Otto, the IRS doesn't like being taken to court. A wildcatter can't operate if anybody looks too closely at his books, and bribes aren't tax deductible. But can you picture Otto worrying about where money comes from or where it's going? He left the bookkeeping and the worrying to me."

Annie glances around the room at the once lavish furnishings that have grown shabby despite Marian's careful tending. "I guess you didn't do too well."

Marian looks too. In her mind, she sees the objects that are no longer here: The flatware and crystal, the Hummel figurines, Annie's piano, Otto's shotguns, the mahogany china and gun cabinets, the Barbie Doll collectibles. She also sees the tax-free bonds, the gold pesos, the emeralds, the sacks of sterling silver coins, and the platinum Rolexes stashed in the floor safe that no one—Otto and the Internal Revenue Service included—knew existed until long after the bankruptcy settlement.

"I did well enough to send you to that fancy university and keep up the payments on Otto's life insurance policy," Marian says. "Oh my God, when I think how you squandered your education, without so much as finding a husband, and what I could do with that money now."

"All right, mother, suppose you had a hundred thousand dollars, roughly the price of my history degree from Southern Methodist. What would you do with it?"

Marian stops her rhythmic motions and looks at Annie, whose arms are crossed under the bikini top. In the way Annie holds herself, in the firm young breasts and long legs that are almost too thin, Marian sees herself—as if she's stepped off the wall, straight out of one of Otto's goddamned slides. But in Annie's face, drawn down in a loose, hurt expression, Marian sees too much of Otto.

"Redecorate the house?" Annie suggests. "Take a trip to the Bahamas? Buy a Lexus? A diamond bracelet? Another set of swords to sharpen?"

Looking into Annie's eyes, Marian says, "I'd buy my freedom. My ticket out of this place and away from the two of you."

Marian beats the sharpener against the sword blade, and the ringing sound jars Otto awake. He looks up blankly as she stands over him, the sword suspended above his head. "For the love of Christ, Marian," he says. "Don't do it."

She drops the sharpener and cuts the air above his head. "Don't be ridiculous." But she's thinking about the life insurance policy that carries an amount nearly as hefty as Otto himself. "You are worth more dead than alive, though. It's tempting."

Otto smiles, as if reassured that she's joking, and rises up in the chair to bring his fat face closer. "How about a kiss from my sweetie?"

The milk of magnesia mustache has dried into amber flakes on Otto's upper lip, and Marian sees clots of the stuff at the corners of his mouth. "Oh no."

"Not even a little one?"

From behind the chair, Annie reaches over to kiss Otto's cheek.

Marian watches them snuggle, Annie's yellow bikini top merging with Otto's stained and bloated pajamas.

"Come on, Marian." Otto holds out a hand. "Join in."

Marian shakes the sword. "I'll kiss you with this."

"That's better than nothing, I guess," Otto says.

Annie frowns up at Marian and loops protective, piña colada arms around Otto—at a place, Marian notes, where ordinary men have necks.

"You wouldn't know it now," Otto says, "but your mother was once my little sweetie. We kissed all the time, and we were tearing off each other's clothes every chance we had."

He turns his head toward Annie but his eyes never leave Marian's. "Does it bother you to hear me talk like this?"

Annie touches his cheek. "No, Daddy, as long as you don't excite yourself."

"It bothers me," Marian says.

Otto looks up at her, eyes drooping, face sagging. "It didn't used to. You couldn't wait till dinner was over. We'd have dessert in bed."

"Otto, stop this now, for God's sake."

As slides of better times flash onto the wall, Marian watches Otto pour Chivas into the glass, add a dollop of milk of magnesia, and stir. The spoon makes its slow ringing, rattling sound. Otto sips, and the sweet, minty odor catches in Marian's throat.

"Beneath the padding," Otto says, "I'm the man I always was."

"Oh really? Should I trim away a few pounds and find out? Nothing major, just a little off the sides." Marian raises the sword over her head and swings downward, as if chopping wood with an ax. "Two whacks and you could be that much closer to your old self, the man I fell in love with. What do you say?"

In Otto's eyes, in the hint of a jaw line above the second chin, Marian thinks she sees traces of Otto the fighter pilot, Otto the lover, Otto the swindler, Otto the wildcatter, Otto the tough and canny enemy of the Internal Revenue Service.

"Start cutting," he says. "If this is what we've come to, what difference does it make?"

Marian clutches the sword so hard her knuckles hurt. "Don't push me, Otto. You don't know how badly I want to."

"Well?" Otto throws out both arms as if to welcome the attack. In the process, he splashes the amber contents of his glass across the living room floor. "Go on."

With a short, quick motion, Marian steps in and thrusts.

No one makes a sound for a moment. Otto is staring down at the sword, sunk a third of its length into his belly. Marian's eyes follow the polished, well-honed blade from Otto's stained pajama top to her hands, wrapped around the hilt.

Annie screams. "You've killed him."

"No she hasn't." Otto grips the blade with both hands. "Marian, sweetie, careful as you can, help me pull it out."

"Quiet," Marian says. "Let me think." She stands poised, ready to either thrust the sword deeper or pull it out. And the longer she hesitates, the less certain she feels about which way she should go. "There's not much blood now. If we yank it out, you'll bleed like a stuck pig."

"I'm not going anywhere with a sword in my belly," Otto says. "And if we get to the emergency room and the cops ask me to explain what happened, what am I supposed to say?"

Mention of the police startles Marian. "You're thinking of pressing charges? Attempted murder, maybe? So your *little sweetie* can spend what's left of her miserable life in a cell?"

"Hell no." Otto raises a hand from the blade to gently stroke her arm. "We need to deal with this here, by ourselves, keep the cops out of it."

"Mother," Annie says feebly, "help Daddy now or I'll go to the police myself."

Marian feels a loosening of tension in her chest and throat and arms. "All right. Go get as many clean towels as you can carry, Annie. And bring the peroxide."

Annie runs from the room.

"Son of a bitch, it hurts," Otto says and surprises Marian by smiling. "Feels hot and cold at the same time, like dry ice."

"I know, Otto." She holds out a hand, which he takes and clings to. "You hold on tight and look at your slides. Drink some of that awful concoction."

Otto nods at the empty glass, which lies on his lap, not far from the wound. "I spilled it."

With one hand, Marian props the glass on the arm of the chair and pours the Chivas. Then she adds a dollop of milk of magnesia, stirs, and puts it to Otto's lips for a long sip. "I'm sorry, Otto."

He pulls his lips away from the glass. "Marian, sweetie?"

135

"What is it, darling?"

"If anything happens tonight—you know, if I die—I want you to know I love you. I've always loved you."

She looks away. "I know you do, Otto, but nothing's going to happen."

"Marian?"

"What is it, Otto?"

"I feel sleepy. Can't keep my eyes open." Otto's head lolls forward and he begins to snore, the rolls of fat expanding and contracting with each breath, the sword hilt moving slowly up and down.

Marian stands, watching him, for a long time. Then, keeping one hand on the sword, she bends down and kisses his slack lips.

Cage

"What do you think of these?" the woman asked.

She placed a wire cage containing a blue and green parrot on the Rock Inn's bar and lifted her blouse to reveal her bare breasts.

Only Peter Hoback and Ernesto Morales, the bartender, noticed the woman because she had her back to the dance floor. The Rock was busy for a Thursday night. A local band played country-western songs on a small stage. Couples in Wranglers and pearl-buttoned shirts two-stepped on the dance floor, each agonizing, slow whirl showing names like Leroy and Hotshot on the backs of belts. A tougher crowd in beards and billed hats surrounded the pool tables. The only other person besides Hoback who sat at the bar, a white-haired man Morales addressed as "Senator," stared into his drink.

Morales said, "You can't do that in here."

The woman waited for an answer from Hoback. "Well?"

Hoback studied the breasts for a long time before he glanced up. Shoulder length dark hair framed a face with high cheekbones and eyes the color of the parrot's pinfeathers. The woman had been crying—judging from the pink and swollen skin around the turquoise eyes—but she was smiling now.

So was Hoback. He wanted to tell her that her breasts were wonderful, but when he opened his mouth to speak, he hiccuped.

"Careful, man," Morales said. "You wouldn't want Alf Applehans to walk in and catch you looking at her like that."

"Alf?"

"My husband," the woman said and let the denim blouse fall. Her lips, as perfect as the breasts, twisted slightly at the corners.

"And the biggest, meanest uranium miner you ever saw," Morales added. "When he ain't kicking ass or playing ball, he runs a power shovel over at Pathfinder."

Hoback nodded, but he went on looking at the woman.

"You don't want any part of Alf Applehans, pal," Morales said. He pointed with a spigot. "Or her."

"The son of a bitch says they're not big enough for him, and I should get a boob job," the woman said. She looked at Hoback. "You know, you have such a kind face. And nice eyes. I've always liked men who had blue eyes and dark hair."

Hoback tried not to blink. "Thank you."

The parrot rang a bell, dangling from a hook at the top of the cage.

"I raised her from a chick," the woman said and smiled. "She's good company on winter days."

Though Hoback knew little about birds, this one looked healthy, its feathers bright and glossy, its black eyes gleaming. Sunflower seeds littered the otherwise clean newspaper that lined the bottom of the cage. The parrot leaned over to ring the bell again with its yellow beak.

"I'm leaving Hardwater tomorrow for my mother's place in Laramie," the woman said. "I need a place to stay tonight."

"Don't do it, man," Morales said. "Not unless you're looking to get your ass whupped."

For a while, Hoback regarded the solemn face of Morales. Then he turned back to the woman, opened his mouth, and hiccuped. A moment later, so did the woman's parrot.

She laughed and rubbed up against Hoback. "I know how to cure the hiccups."

"So do I," Morales said. "You bend over and drink a beer upside down."

The woman shook her head. Her parrot hiccuped again.

The senator rapped the bottom of his glass against the bar. "Morales, my boy, I'll have another double Beefeater's. And I believe I'll sample your pickled eggs, if you wouldn't mind fetching me one." When Morales came back, he said, "My grandmother taught me this one. You take three deep breaths, hold the last one, tuck your chin down like this, and stick out your tongue. Works every time. Go ahead, Hoback, try it."

Hoback tried it. This time, when he hiccuped, he nearly bit off his tongue.

"That's not how you cure the hiccups," the woman said.

Morales looked at her. "You close your eyes, put your thumb in your mouth, blow as hard as you can, and pretend you're drowning?"

He rolled his eyes. "Okay, then you get a dude that's maybe six-eight and three hundred pounds—you know, like your husband?—to hold Hoback upside down by the ankles and bang his head against the floor."

"Let me show you," the woman said. She put her arms around Hoback's neck, pulled his face down to hers, and kissed him.

When she let Hoback go, he looked into her eyes and didn't have to pretend he was drowning. Hiccups cured, he bent to kiss her again, but she drew back.

"Dance with me," she said.

As a rule, Hoback didn't dance with married women. As a rule, he didn't kiss them either. They joined the other couples who danced on the worn floorboards to the band's rendition of Willie Nelson's "Good Hearted Woman." She hooked an elbow—snug and possessive—around the back of Hoback's neck. "I'm Carla."

Hoback told her his name.

"Do you have a girlfriend, Peter?" she asked.

He shook his head. "I've only been in Hardwater for a few months."

A couple of weeks ago, a friend had set him up with a mousy girl, Peggy something, with stringy hair, who chain-smoked and laughed at everything he said. She wasn't bad for Hardwater, whose single women could pick from among the three thousand muscular, well-paid young men who worked in the nearby uranium mines, but Hoback had refused all further offers of blind dates.

"So you haven't been here long enough to begin hating the place," Carla said. "To appreciate Hardwater, you have to be trapped here for years, married to your high school sweetheart. You have to bowl Monday nights and play softball on Saturdays with the same people every season. You have to celebrate birthdays at Denny's and anniversaries at the Sizzler. You have to give up your dreams."

They drifted to the rear of the bar, whose wall of weathered pine bore the mounted head of a jackalope—a large jack rabbit fitted with an antelope's antlers—and dusty pictures of famous Wyoming boys like James Watt, Alan Simpson, Jay Novacek, and the white-haired man who drank Beefeater's and ate pickled eggs. Carla turned her face into his shoulder and held on tight. As the couples did their slow whirls, Hoback caught a glimpse of the parrot's cage on the bar.

He speculated about Carla's dreams, afraid to ask about them in case they involved exotic dancing or stand-up comedy.

"I want to be an architect," she said. "As a kid, I couldn't draw people, but I was always great at buildings. I'd draw houses, floor to ceiling, every detail."

She wanted to go to the school of architectural engineering at the University of Wyoming, she said, where she had planned to study before she married Alf.

Hoback saw architecture as sensible enough. "Why wait? Why not go tonight?"

"I'm taking the five-thirty bus. The pickup's in Alf's name. It's our only vehicle, and he needs it for work."

"If you're serious about leaving, about going to school, I'll take you to Laramie right now. My car's out front. You'll be there in four hours."

"Don't you have to work in the morning?"

"If we leave now," he said, "I can be back in Hardwater by dawn."

"You'd do that for me?"

She pulled him down for another kiss with hiccup-curing power. Before they finished, the Rock Inn's front door opened. At the sound, Carla pushed Hoback away and flattened against the wall, jiggling the photographs.

Hoback faced the door with his hands up. Three young men in the dirty jeans and work shirts of uranium miners came into the bar and shouted at a cluster of pool players. Pointing at the parrot on the bar, they laughed and took stools near the senator.

"Jesus Christ."

"Sorry." Carla pushed away from the wall. "I thought it was Alf."

Hoback had a clear image of a three hundred-pound body crushing him to the floor while Carla moved out of the way.

"It's time to get on the road," he said.

At the bar, Carla excused herself and made her way past the pool tables to the rest room. Hoback glanced up to find Morales watching him.

"I'm driving her to Laramie," Hoback said. "I'll be back in time for work in the morning."

Morales filled a shot glass with beer and held it up to the birdcage. The parrot leaned against the wire bars to dip its beak in the shot glass, which Morales tilted gently. "My friend here loves Coors," he said. "While you been romancing Alf Applehans's wife, I been getting to know the family pet. Want to hear her talk?"

Though Hoback showed little interest, Morales coaxed the bird to speak by threatening to hold back the beer. "Carlie loves Alfie," the parrot said.

"Have some Coors, Pepita," Morales said. "Pepita the Parrot, that's what I call her. Beats hell out of whatever those Anglos call you, uh Pepita?"

"Carla feels trapped living here in Hardwater," Hoback said. "She always wanted to be an architect, and there's a good school of architectural engineering at UW. She'll study there and live with her mother. I'm driving her to Laramie, Ernesto. That's all there is to it."

Morales nodded in a way Hoback didn't like and poured Pepita another shot. "Yeah, that's all there is to it, except I saw how you looked at her tits. You want to believe this do-gooder horseshit, Hoback, that's up to you, but don't expect me to believe it."

Hoback glanced at the door to the women's room then up at the glowing Coors clock above the bar. "What's keeping her?"

"Come on, Pepita." Morales offered the parrot another drink. "Talk to me, girl."

"Carlie loves Alfie."

As Morales laughed, the Rock Inn's front door swung open and banged against the wall. A man with shoulders as wide as the doorway stopped just inside to scan the room. Dressed in faded denim and a pair of black ropers that Hoback could have used as skis, he had a massive forehead and rounded cheeks that made his mouth, nose, and eyes look small—packed into the center of his face. But Hoback's gaze settled on the baby, fat and blond, who rode in a nylon contraption—like a kangaroo's pouch—slung across the man's chest. From the pouch, the baby looked into the room with round, startled eyes.

"Oh shit," Morales said.

Pepita the Parrot spoke, without a bribe, of Carlie's love for Alfie. As Alf Applehans approached the bar, the baby, catching sight of the bird, gave a toothless grin and tried to reach for the cage.

"Uh, Alf," the bartender said, "you know you can't bring the kid in here."

Applehans had blond sideburns and a mustache so white it was almost transparent. His blue eyes, set deep in his wide face, squinted down at Hoback and Morales. "Where is she?"

For an instant, Hoback considered lying. "In the ladies' room, getting ready to go to Laramie," he said. "I've offered to drive her to her mother's."

Applehans drew in a breath and let it out slowly. "Carla's not going to Laramie."

Morales reached across the bar to clap a hand on Hoback's shoulder, but Hoback got to his feet. "I promised to take her," he said, his voice quivering. "I didn't know about the baby."

Applehans shrugged his heavy shoulders. The baby's head bobbed up and down, but his round eyes never left the parrot. "Carla's not going because she never goes. Every year we have a bad fight, and she talks about leaving Hardwater. And every year she finds some poor, dumb bastard like you to promise he'll take her somewhere. And every year I have to knock the poor, dumb bastard's teeth down his throat so we can go home and get some sleep. Only this year you're one lucky poor, dumb bastard because whatever my wife decides to do, I won't beat a man in front of my son."

Hoback sat down on his stool and watched Pepita ring her bell until the senator spoke to Applehans. "How's my favorite constituent?" the senator asked, lisping the T's. A full set of dentures lay on the bar next to his empty glass. "Would you care for a drink, my boy?"

"No," Applehans said.

At that moment, Carla returned to stand beside Hoback's stool.

"Can we go home now?" Applehans asked.

"I am going home," she said. "To Laramie."

Applehans nodded slowly. "You'll need some extra money. Take this. I'll send you more on payday."

She hesitated before accepting a silver clip of folded bills, which she slipped into her purse.

"And I thought you might like to have this to remember Alfie by," he said and handed her a framed photograph of the baby.

Carla looked at the photograph for a moment. "You son of a bitch." She began throwing hard, one-handed punches at Applehans, who hunched his shoulders and turned his back to cover the baby. "I wanted to be an architect. I didn't want a child yet. I told you that. And now I love him too much. You son of a bitch."

The baby was crying, and so was Carla. She stopped punching Applehans and held out her arms. "Give him to me."

After some hesitation, Applehans undid the safety straps, gently drew Alfie out of the kangaroo pouch, and handed him over. The baby waved his fat arms in the air, his eyes clamped shut, his face turning a dark shade of red. Carla hugged him to her chest and kissed him until he stopped crying.

"I'm taking him with me," she said.

Applehans reached out as if to snatch back his son, but his big hands stopped just short of the baby. Then he let his arms fall to his sides.

"Come with us, Alf," Carla said. "You can find a job in Laramie until I finish school. We can start fresh."

"My work is here," he said with a heavy shrug. "My life is here. And so is yours."

Carla shook her head. "Not anymore."

She went to the bar and picked up the parrot's cage. After looking at the parrot for a long time, she handed the cage to Applehans, who held it clumsily. "You know how much I love her," Carla said. "She got me through a lot of lonely times. I want you to keep her. Talk to her."

Carla turned to Hoback. "Can we go now?"

Looking into Applehans's sad, deep-set eyes, Hoback was afraid he might see tears. Instead, Applehans shifted the cage to one hand and pointed a thick finger at Hoback.

"You and me and your teeth," Applehans said. "Tomorrow night."

Hoback nodded, but he was thinking he'd like to keep his teeth. He was thinking he might stay in Laramie for a while—find a job, start fresh, get to know Carla better. He was thinking he'd lived in Hardwater long enough to appreciate it.

Purple Heart

It took divorce and financial ruin to get Jim Pickett to ask his father for help.

He made the first plea after Evelyn emptied their checking account and drove away in their new Odyssey. Her parting note read, "I no longer want to be married to you. I'm keeping the Honda. You keep the house, the pickup, and the kids."

The checks for the mortgage, the electric bill, and the MasterCard cleared before Evelyn robbed the bank on her way out of Fort Worth. The community college paid Pickett monthly, and he had two boys to feed. Hocking his mountain bike got them through the first week. Hocking his kayak got them through the second. Visits to Coin-Star and Half-Price Books got them through half of the third week, but then he called his father, Leo, and asked to borrow four hundred bucks.

The money arrived by Fed-Ex, with a note that read, "Jim, I'm sorry to hear you and Evelyn are having trouble. I can't afford to give you money every month, so get your finances in order, even if this means asking your creditors to restructure your payments. Love, Dad."

Pickett wadded the note and four new hundred-dollar bills into a ball, which he threw across the room. An hour later, he found the money and took the boys to Jack in the Box.

He intended never to ask Leo for help again, but that was before the pickup started trailing blue smoke. In an e-mail, Leo mentioned plans to buy a new Acura, so Pickett called to ask what he planned to do with his old Caravan.

"I'm going to trade it in on the Acura."

"Why don't you find out how much they'll give you for the trade-in and sell it to me for the same price?"

Leo hesitated as if his son were asking for another handout. "I thought you were broke."

"I'm doing okay now, Dad. Feel free to add the four hundred you loaned me to the price of the van."

A couple of freelance editing jobs had returned Pickett to solvency. He also learned to cook rice, beans, vegetables, pasta, potatoes—anything he could boil or microwave. That meant fewer trips to Jack in the Box and

145

a better cash flow. He had a few hundred dollars left over at the end of each month. So every night after Bart and Drew went to bed, he took consolation—when he wasn't weeping into his pillow—that they would survive.

Leo planned to attend a reunion of his infantry regiment in Nashville, so he offered to let Pickett and the boys hitch a ride from Fort Worth to his home in Carmel, where they could pick up the van and drive it back to Texas. "Might give my grandsons and me a chance to bond," Leo said. "Get to know each other better."

Until they settled into the aromatic leather seats of the Acura, Pickett thought the trip might also give him, the cuckolded community college journalism teacher, and his father, two years a widower, a chance to bond. But the first thing Leo said as they pulled out of Pickett's driveway was "You don't want to ask to drive my new car."

"I wouldn't think of it."

In truth, Pickett lusted to feel under his foot the surge of the Acura's supercharged engine, but he recalled too well, even after twenty-five years, Leo's tough-love driving lessons. These involved Leo rewarding Pickett's fumbling first attempts to shift gears—and the inevitable engine stalls—with repeated punches to the same spot on his shifting arm. By the time his first lesson ended, Pickett couldn't lift his arm, much less shift gears. In the event that he committed some unforgivable offense with the Acura—hit a pothole or changed lanes too fast—he did not want the boys to see their grandfather tattoo a driving lesson on his arm.

As they sped along Interstate 40 toward Santa Rosa, Pickett recalled his mother's patient advice on how to operate a standard transmission and her wild cover stories for the dents he put in the family Jeep. She served as a buffer between Leo and their children, moving chairs to cover chocolate stains on the carpet, turning a broken camera into a missing camera, insisting he show the family all the affection and respect he could muster. She stayed in touch with the kids after she and Leo left the homestead in Colorado and retired to Carmel, near the golfing Mecca of Pebble Beach. She made everyone's life happier, and her death left Leo alone with his satellite dish, his golf rounds, and his regimental reunions.

As the Llano Estacado slid by outside the car, Pickett wondered if Leo missed her as much as he did. Her death had left a hole in his life at least as big as the one left by Evelyn. And it meant the boys had one fewer person to love them—someone who could have eased the pain of desertion.

"Do you ever think about Mom?"

Leo glanced at Pickett. "I don't want to talk about her."

"What do you want to talk about?"

Leo turned back to the road. "I want to drive my car."

On vacations, when Evelyn and Pickett loved each other, they often stopped for lunch at the old-fashioned coffee shop at Cline's Corner and let the boys pick out a souvenir from among the gift shop's stock of crystals, arrowheads, bolo ties, kachina dolls, rubber tomahawks, and key rings.

Each smell of the place—bacon, fudge, new leather, rubber, lacquered pine, dirty diapers—carried a memory of past trips: Evelyn's smile as Bart tried on a five-gallon hat, four gallons too big; Drew, as a toddler, gripping an action figure with such strength they had to buy it for him or turn him into a shoplifter; Evelyn's indulgence of her lust for turquoise jewelry. Cline's Corner was their jumping off place, a sign they had left Texas, thank God, and were half a day's drive from Colorado's aspen groves or Utah's slickrock paradise.

Most years, Pickett's heart would flutter in anticipation of the first glimpse of the Rockies, where he and Evelyn had met and lived for the first ten years of their marriage. This year, as he, Leo, and the boys took a booth at the coffee shop, his heart was pounding not fluttering. Instead of bonding with his grandsons, Leo sipped coffee and read *Forbes*, his face ruddy under his thinning white hair, his lips compressed into a slight frown, his eyes clear and hard as they scanned an article on hedge funds. Leo's silences during meals had made Pickett anxious from birth. A certified public accountant, Leo made a career of keeping his clients' financial affairs a secret. He was good enough at his job to retire early and well. Only Pickett's mother knew how to draw him into the conversations, using the right mix of topic, charm, and phrasing. Pickett had worked for nine years as a magazine reporter, able to persuade the most reticent of sources to talk, but Leo was impervious to interviewing techniques. So they sat in silence at the table, the boys eating BLTs and sipping from oversized glasses of milk until, reaching for a napkin, Bart knocked over Drew's glass, spilling the contents across the tabletop and onto Leo's copy of *Forbes*.

"Oh, for Christ's sake," Leo rumbled. "What the hell are you thinking, boy?"

Bart looked up, his dark eyes wide with panic. "I didn't do it."

Leo shook the milk off the article he was reading and checked his navy polo for stains. "What do you mean you didn't do it? I sat here and watched you knock the glass over."

Bart sat frozen in the face of his grandfather's stare, his eyes filling with tears. Beside him, Drew held a similar pose, his expression wary but curious. The boys looked like different-sized versions of each other. They had Evelyn's high cheek bones, wide mouths, straight noses, and large, brown eyes—most of what made them good to look at. They also had Pickett's dark hair, which they wore shaggy to hide their ears—his most obvious contribution to their genetic makeup. Bart said, "I mean, I d-didn't mean to d-do it."

Pickett put a hand on Bart's shoulder. "Don't worry about it, Buddy. We'll get it cleaned up. Why don't you and Drew go pick out a toy? We'll pay for lunch and join you in a second."

The boys vanished into the gift shop. Pickett sopped up milk with a handful of napkins and leaned across the table to get his father's full attention. "I'd appreciate it, Dad, if you wouldn't yell at the boys. Or make them out to be liars."

Leo jerked back, as if Pickett's anger startled him. "Bart did lie, plain and simple."

Pickett threw the sodden napkins onto Bart's plate and grabbed another handful. "Yes, he lied and he stuttered, for the plain and simple reason that you scared the shit out of him."

A look of alarm crossed Leo's face.

"And when I was a kid you scared the shit out of me."

For a moment they regarded each other in silence. Then Leo gave a pained shrug. "I guess I'm not too good with kids."

The understatement caught Pickett unawares. Leo's grin, which softened his face, was so rare an event that, in spite of his anger, Pickett smiled back at him. "Maybe we should catch up to the boys before they tear up the gift shop."

Leo insisted on paying the check. Pickett let him.

In the toy section, the boys had narrowed their choices to high-pressure squirt guns and wooden boomerangs. The squirt guns looked like trouble. Pickett had a clear mental image of Drew soaking the back of his grandfather's balding head as they cruised west along I-40.

Leo caught them at the gift shop cash register. He eyed the boomerangs, but if he disapproved of the purchase he kept quiet. The boomerangs—tan and red—reminded Pickett of one he had as a kid. When Leo stopped for the night, maybe the boomerangs would give the boys something active to do.

In the parking lot, gripping the boomerangs like swords, Bart and Drew traded Hollywood-style saber blows until Bart hit Drew on the finger. With a deep-throated roar, Drew dealt his big brother a blow to the side of the head. In response, Bart lifted his boomerang in both hands, like a sledgehammer. Pickett interrupted the swing and confiscated both weapons, which went into the Acura's trunk.

As they got into the car, Leo said, "I could have told you boomerangs were a bad idea—if you'd asked."

In a motel near Grants, New Mexico, Leo settled into a queen-sized bed and switched on the rebroadcast of a PGA tournament on ESPN. The boys jumped on the other bed and shouted, "Nickelodeon, Nickelodeon."

To keep a lid on Leo's temper, Pickett took the boys to an empty lot beyond the motel parking lot to try their boomerangs.

Mount Taylor, a dormant volcano, rose above Grants, and the sight of it distracted him. One winter, a short time after their marriage, Evelyn and Pickett skied to the top of Mount Taylor, where they sat on the summit and took in the vistas of New Mexico. On the descent, they telemarked down an open snowfield, their graceful S-turns the only blot on the pristine landscape until Pickett caught a tip and fell. The spruce and pines on the upper slopes of the mountain looked like snow sculptures, every needle sheathed in ice. All the way down, they smiled at each other out of a shared sense of wonder and joy. The memory of that time, like so many others from their marriage, left Pickett feeling hollow and confused at the cold, undeniable reality that Evelyn had left him, left their boys.

Drew brought him back to the moment. "Give me my boomerang."

"Me too," Bart said.

Drew's first throw sent his boomerang on a straight, tumbling course into the brush at the edge of the lot. He charged after it. Bart threw side-armed, and his boomerang hooked before dropping near a Days Inn billboard. As Bart worked at perfecting his technique, each time getting a few degrees closer to a circular throw, Drew watched his brother's success with a baleful glare. Each of Drew's failed throws brought a harsh cry. Finally, having decided the fault lay with the boomerang, he offered to trade with Bart. Bart agreed to the trade, for the moment avoiding trouble.

When Bart's boomerang worked no better than his own, Drew flung it away and dropped to his knees in the dirt of the lot, his small body wracked with sobs.

Between breaths, he choked out, "I can't do it."

Drew's learning style—trial, failure, raging breakdown—had to run its course before he would listen to instruction. Pickett had explained this fact to Drew's kindergarten teacher, a kind and patient woman who often reached the limits of kindness and patience with Drew. Now, Drew listened, his gaze intense, as Pickett demonstrated the technique.

On his next throw, the boomerang curved back toward them. As Drew ran after it, the tears still drying on his face, he laughed out loud. Before long, Pickett watched as both boys made curving throws.

Confident now, they continued to throw their boomerangs even as they walked back toward the hotel. Pickett was about to warn them they were getting too close when Drew's boomerang slipped from his hand and flew toward Leo's Acura. Their bodies jerked at the impact.

"Shit." The word slipped out before Pickett could stop it. "Well, we didn't need this."

They stood there, looking at each other.

"Nice one, stupid!" Bart said. Drew tried to hit him.

Pickett went over to have a look. In the reflected light from the motel room, he could see the dent, small but definite, in the middle of the passenger door—the only blot on an otherwise pristine surface.

Before dawn, Bart sat up in bed and screamed "Mommy!"

Pickett came off the mattress in one move, his hands up like a boxer's.

Bart wept and muttered and shrieked; Drew wept in harmony. From under his covers Leo groaned, "What in God's name? They'll wake the whole goddamned motel."

Pickett switched on a bedside lamp. Bart stared at the motel room door, a look of horror on his face, as if he saw something large and reptilian.

"Night terrors," Pickett explained. "He gets them every few days. Scares the living shit out of me every time."

Leo pulled a pillow over his head. "Can't you get him to stop?"

The night terrors had to run their course, according Bart's pediatric counselor, but to satisfy his own parental instincts and appease Leo—who would need his sleep to cope with the discovery, in a few hours, of the dent in his Acura—Pickett stroked Bart's hair. "Quiet down now, Buddy, everything's all right," he whispered. With his free hand, he patted Drew's back. Drew soon fell asleep, but Bart went on staring at unseen monsters, trembling and calling out for his mother.

In the weeks after Evelyn left, long after bedtime, Pickett would sometimes wake to hear Bart crying in his room and go in to comfort him. One night, he could not console him. When he asked what was wrong, Bart didn't answer for a long time. Then he let out a strangled wail: "Mommy doesn't love me."

His words bore a bleak truth. Evelyn had doted on Drew, never missing a chance to touch and kiss him, telling her friends about every funny thing he said, buying him the candy, toys, books, and clothes he demanded in his gruff voice. She never pushed Bart away, but she left him for Pickett to love.

"Of course she loves you. She's confused about who she is and what she's doing, that's all. She left because she no longer wanted to be married to me. It had nothing to do with you."

At the time, he put into the speech all the gravity he could muster, but he could see Bart didn't buy it. His young face had revealed his thoughts as clearly as if he had spoken them, and they spoke for Pickett as much as they did for him: If she loves me, how could she leave me? All Pickett knew to do was to hug his son and tell him he loved him.

This night's terrors ended with an anticlimactic nod, Bart's dark hair scattered across his forehead. Then his eyes lolled shut, and Pickett guided his head to the pillow. He reached for the light switch.

Leo asked, "Did the nightmares start when Evelyn ran off?"

Pickett turned to face his father. "He used to get them before kindergarten, but we thought he'd outgrown them. And as you'll no doubt see in the morning, Drew's started wetting the bed again. It's a mess, but please don't mention it. If anyone asks about the yellow stain, he claims it's from sweat."

The corners of Leo's mouth twitched. "And you think it's a good idea to let him pretend there's no problem?"

"Even at six he needs his pride, Dad. And rubbing someone's nose in it isn't always the answer."

Leo closed his eyes and sighed. "Did I say you should rub his nose in it? Maybe he needs to talk to a shrink."

Pickett fought the urge to roll his eyes like a teenager. "He saw the same counselor as Bart and spent four sessions hammering nails in the play therapy room. To the counselor this indicated he was harboring anger, which was quite a revelation for a hundred bucks an hour."

"So where does that leave you?"

"I'm supposed to give Drew opportunities to express his anger. And I'm supposed to give both boys plenty of hugs, which is easy because they're loveable little guys. Oh, and I'm supposed to reassure them that their mother still loves them in spite of the fact that she ran off to Georgia to start a new life with a shit-kicker named Cliff."

"Have you heard from her?"

"Twice in five months."

A few weeks after she left, Evelyn phoned to give Pickett a forwarding address for her mail. She had no plans to come to Texas except to finalize the divorce, and she did not ask to talk to the boys. Two months later, fragile and tentative, she called again to ask if she could please speak to Drew and Bart. The conversation left both boys smiling and bouncing around the house. "Mommy's coming home," Bart shouted. When he handed Pickett the phone, Evelyn said it was all a mistake; she wanted to make their marriage work; she wanted to be a mother again; she wanted to know if he could see it in his heart to take her back. "Come home, and we'll see," Pickett said, but any hope raised by the call died in the silence that followed. If Evelyn failed to request regular visitation rights within six months, Texas law would grant him full custody of the boys and force her to pay child support. Evelyn was a CPA, like Leo, so if she chose to stay in Georgia with Cliff the support would be substantial. It was cold comfort, as he told Leo now, but it might cover future nail-hammering sessions for Drew.

Leo gave a grunt of disgust. "I'll never understand how the woman I thought I knew, and loved like a daughter, could run off and leave her own children." After a pause, he added, "Well, let's get some shuteye, son. It's Barstow or bust by tomorrow night."

Morning brought the discovery of stained sheets.

Drew's eyes shifted from face to face, ready to correct any misconceptions about bedwetting, and with a fixed stare Pickett urged Bart to keep quiet.

"These motel rooms get pretty hot at night," Leo offered. "It's a wonder I didn't soak my sheets."

Drew nodded. "Yeah."

Leo's show of sensitivity lulled Pickett into a false sense of confidence. During the night, he considered blaming another driver's carelessness for the dent in the Acura's door. Now, he decided to own up.

"Uh, Dad, maybe you'd better come outside and take a look at your car."

Leo froze in the act of putting on a pair of golf pants, his expression shifting from kindly to suspicious. "Why?"

Pickett told him. Shirtless and silent, Leo left the room and walked around the Acura. "Get dressed," Pickett told the boys and went outside. Leo knelt by the car door, his thinning white hair blowing in the slight breeze. As Leo straightened, Pickett noticed the withered muscles of his torso and the faded blue and red tattoo of his regimental insignia on his shoulder.

"I'll pay for the damages."

Leo gave a short, humorless laugh. "You're going to pay fifteen hundred bucks, counting paint and body work, on your salary?"

There was nothing to say. Leo was right. Fifteen hundred bucks was beyond him—four or five months' careful savings. As he stood there, Pickett thought back to his twelfth birthday, when Leo gave him a copy of Horatio Alger's *Ragged Dick* and a professional shoeshine kit. Pickett had hoped for a bicycle. Still, he got the message: at twelve, he should look for a job. To make Leo proud, he spent the next year rising before dawn and walking through the cold and dark to deliver the *Denver Post* to sixty neighbors. He spent the rest of his childhood cleaning up construction sites and mowing the fairways at Leo's country club. Leo expected his eldest son to follow him into accounting, but in college Pickett decided to pursue work in newspapers, even if doing so meant earning a lower salary for longer hours. When he married Evelyn, the profession she and Leo shared gave them a special bond—and, as he later realized, a shared contempt for his work as a journalist.

He saw the contempt in Leo's face now.

"At least let me pay the deductible."

With a wave of his hand, Leo said, "You had the guts to admit it. That's more than your mother let you do when you used to wreck my cars."

He studied Pickett's face. "Of course I knew. I loved the woman, so I let her think she was fooling me."

"Sorry about the door."

Almost gently, Leo said, "It's not the money, Jim. It's that—suddenly—my new car's no longer new." He slapped an open hand against the dented door and went inside.

The boys made it through breakfast at Denny's without spilling their milk, but their complaints started at the Arizona line.

"When can we stop?" Bart asked.

Leo's tone was flat and precise: "We'll have lunch in Flagstaff."

Drew wadded up the picture he was coloring. "I'm bored."

Leo breathed deeply, perhaps trying to lower his blood pressure. "Look at the scenery."

To occupy the boys, Pickett had Bart show Drew their location on the road map, but the plan backfired. At the sight of Flagstaff, still half a state away, Bart's face fell, and even to Pickett the town of Barstow looked too far west to make by nightfall. Then Bart began to notice the many national parks and monuments, outlined in heavy green lines, along their route.

He put his finger on a point near the border. "Can we see the Painted Desert?"

Leo kept his eyes on the road.

"Not this trip," Pickett said.

"The Petrified Forest?"

"No."

"The Meteor Crater?" Bart's voice grew more strident with each question. "The Grand Canyon?"

"Maybe we'll see the Grand Canyon on the way home."

Drew began kicking the back of Leo's seat.

"Hey." Pickett reached back to touch Drew's knee. "Why don't you sit still for a while?"

"Because I don't want to."

"Son," Pickett warned.

Drew kicked the seat again. "I don't want to."

That's when Leo erupted. "Drew!" He half turned in the driver's seat, his eyes showing the whites. "Stop your kicking."

As a boy, faced with such anger, Pickett would have cringed or cried. But Drew's wide mouth firmed into a single line and his brown eyes turned as hard as polished maple. He kicked the back of Leo's seat with a violent thump. "I don't want to!"

Instead of exploding into rage, maybe killing them all by swerving off the highway at eighty miles per hour, Leo laughed. "That boy's a pistol. Just like his grandpa."

Disaster averted. Leo refocused his attention on the road. Bart regarded Leo with a solemn expression. Like Pickett, yelling made him cringe. Like Pickett, Bart was no pistol. Like Pickett, he appeared to be thinking, "So this is our family vacation?"

And he was right. Driving across the West in a closed car with Leo Pickett was no vacation. To Leo, Pickett said, "We should stop somewhere and let the boys run around."

Leo kept his eyes on the road. "If we're going to make Carmel in three days—and get you your van—we can't stop every five minutes. We'll stop for lunch in Flagstaff."

Pickett unhooked his seatbelt and faced the boys. "You guys remember your grandma, right? She used to love family vacations, especially in the Rockies. You know what we'd be doing right now if she were with us?"

Bart looked at him. Drew kept coloring and kicking the back of Leo's seat. Leo bent more deeply over the steering wheel.

"We'd have to explore every Jeep road we saw, stopping to collect rusted lengths of barbed wire, chunks of petrified wood, or weathered tree stumps. Once, we had to carry a stump for half a mile so she could put it in her garden. I must have been your age, Bart. It felt like we'd never get to the station wagon, and when we did the stump was so big we couldn't get it into the cargo area. We had to tie it on top, and every time we passed a car, people pointed at us and laughed."

His face blank, Leo glanced over. "I told you I didn't want to talk about her."

"Then don't talk." Pickett directed his words to his boys. "Grandma was a lot of fun, but her cooking was an adventure because she didn't follow recipes. Her key lime pie never set right. It would ooze off the crust when you cut it, so we used to call it 'key slime pie.'"

Bart smiled tentatively. "I remember that."

Drew's expression turned somber. "Grandma got cancer from smoking cigarettes."

The car slowed, and Leo took an exit ramp leading to a desolate-looking ranch road, paved for fifty yards before it turned into dirt. He stopped at the end of the pavement, unbuckled his seatbelt, got out of the car, and slammed his door shut.

"Stay here," Pickett told the boys.

Leo stood before a barbed-wire fence, gripping the top strand in both hands. In the distance, a sandstone mesa towered above the small dome of a Navajo hogan. A lean Appaloosa browsed a pasture of sage and sparse grass.

"She's my mother and the boys' grandmother. Why the hell can't we talk about her?"

Leo let go of the barbed wire to make a short, chopping motion with his hand. "You're riding in my car, and I asked you not to."

They watched the Appaloosa graze. When the silence threatened to stretch to the horizon, Leo turned to face Pickett. "Missing Katherine has left an ache in my gut that I'll take to my grave, but she's gone. Talking about her hurts too much, okay?"

Bart and Drew appeared at Pickett's elbow. "We need to pee."

As it happened, so did their father and grandfather. Standing in a row near the fence, the Picketts engaged in a multi-generational pissing contest. Then the boys ran along the fence line, pelting each other with dirt clods until Leo put an end to the rest break.

Back on the highway, the boys played twenty questions for a while, but the objects Bart chose—the galaxy, a smile, oxygen, DNA—infuriated Drew. To avoid a pitched battle in the backseat, Pickett searched for something that might entertain them, and his heel hit an object under the seat. He bent and brought up a polished wooden box that he recognized. It contained the medals Leo earned more than half a century earlier in amphibious battles for Pacific islands. The medals had fascinated Pickett as a child; they made his father someone special. He took pride in Leo's courage and, at the same time, asked himself the unsettling question of how he would have behaved under fire. No matter how much his children pestered him, Leo refused to talk about how he won the medals. From their mother, Pickett knew about a dead Japanese soldier in the Philippines and a squad of pinned-down soldiers he saved in New Guinea.

"Mind if I show the boys?" Pickett asked.

Leo hesitated. "The reunion organizers asked us to bring our decorations. It's embarrassing. The heroes died in combat. The rest of us made it by dumb luck or by keeping our heads down."

The boys gazed at the medals. Bart asked, "What are they for?"

Leo gave the standard answer: "Being in the wrong place at the wrong time."

So Pickett told the stories as his mother had told them, leaving it up to Leo to alter or add details if he felt the need. At the wheel, Leo stiffened at the description of his wild charge up a grassy slope, in the teeth of withering machine-gun fire, which earned him the Bronze Star.

The boys touched the medals, and Bart kept looking from the gold profile of George Washington, silhouetted by deep purple glass, on the Purple Heart to the profile of his grandfather. Pickett watched his older son's face awaken to the wonder of having a war hero in the family.

Leo glanced back at Bart's admiring expression with a troubled frown. He lifted a hand from the wheel and made a half-hearted gesture, as if trying to find the right words. "Listen, I don't want them getting the wrong idea about this war hero nonsense."

"What do you mean?"

He looked uncomfortable. "Your mother loved me, and she wanted our children to think well of me."

Pickett stared at Leo's profile. "Are you telling me she made it up?"

Leo shook his head. "No, but reality isn't so simple or pretty. And I wasn't Audie Murphy."

Leo drove in silence for several miles, leaving Pickett to puzzle over how much license his mother had taken with the truth. "I ran up the slope," Leo finally said. "That's true enough. But I was shell-shocked—scared out of my wits—and in the confusion I guess I ran toward instead of away from the enemy. The other guys followed me, and one of them took out the machine-gun. That's the truth about my Bronze Star." He grinned for an instant. "Not very heroic, is it?"

Arizona flashed by—cliffs of red sandstone, sagebrush flats cut by arroyos, distant mesa tops crowned by piñon-juniper forests. But Pickett was looking beyond the mesa tops to a hillside on the embattled island of New Guinea decades earlier—at a young soldier who risked death by charging without fear through the tall grass. This image gave way to that of a young man too terrified and confused to realize he was running the wrong way.

"Sorry to disappoint you, son."

He sounded so earnest Pickett had to shake his head. "I'm glad you told me. What about the Purple Heart?"

Leo closed his eyes for a moment, and the corners of his mouth turned down in disgust or sadness. "A young Japanese soldier shot me. Shooting him back was automatic—no time to think, or get scared, or feel sick until after it was over. So he never went home to finish school, fall in love, start a family, and live his life."

"If you hadn't—" Pickett glanced at his sons in the backseat.

Leo nodded and let his shoulders sag. The conversation Pickett had sought for most of his life was over. Leo had given what he could, told Pickett what he could stand to tell.

"Grandpa?" Drew asked.

"Yes, Drew?"

He kicked the back of Leo's seat. "Are we almost to Flagstaff?"

Before they reached Flagstaff, just outside the small town of Winslow, Leo pulled off the highway at an exit leading to the famous Barringer Meteor Crater. "Let's give the boys a chance to stretch their legs."

Both boys sat up in their seats, eyes wide with excitement at the unexpected stop. The road to the crater ran in a straight line for several miles before snaking up the steep slope created by the impact of the meteorite. Pickett's mother, who had loved geological wonders almost as much as weathered stumps, insisted on stopping at the meteor crater every time they passed through Arizona. It was a family tradition, and stopping here meant more to Leo—and to Pickett—than a chance for the boys to stretch their legs.

Tour buses and recreational vehicles crowded the parking lot. Bart and Drew were so eager to get out of the car that Leo dropped his passengers at the ticket booth before finding a parking space. Pickett held his sons by the hand until they reached the window, where he bought admission for four. The boys amused themselves by climbing on the metal handrails lining the path until Leo caught up with them. He reached for his wallet.

"I've got your ticket, Dad."

Leo accepted it with a tentative smile. He blinked for a moment, as if to get his bearings.

Since their last visit to the crater, the museum had added an impressive looking coffee shop, a planetary science wing, an interactive exhibit with sample meteorites, and displays that used computer graphics to illustrate such phenomena as the energy released by the meteorite's impact—a thousand times greater than the bomb that obliterated Hiroshima. The boys went straight to the computerized displays, pressing buttons to watch the meteorite explode over and over again.

"If you're in a hurry, Dad, we can skip all this."

Leo's lips drew down at the corners, and he shook his head. "I guess Carmel won't vanish if we get there a day late."

He went out the glass doors to the observation decks perched on the rim of the crater. Half an hour later, when the boys had all the interactive learning they could tolerate, they found Leo on a wooden platform that extended over the lip of the crater—a mile wide and six hundred feet deep. He leaned against the metal handrails, staring into the abyss. As Pickett came up beside him, gripping each boy by the hand to prevent their inevitable attempts to climb the handrails, he saw traces of tears in Leo's eyes. Leo brushed his hand across his face and slung an arm over Pickett's shoulders.

Surprised, Pickett let go of Bart to pat Leo's back. "The boys want to look through the telescope at the top of the trail and then eat lunch."

"First, I have something for you." Leo took an object out of his pocket and held it in his closed fist. "As the eldest son, you'd get this one day anyway."

On Pickett's T-shirt, over the left side of his chest, Leo pinned his Purple Heart.

"This is for surviving wounds suffered in love not war. I wish I had one for each of you. Call it a unit citation; it belongs to the three of you."

They all stared, dazzled by the sight of the medal, which turned the bright Arizona sun into beams of gold and purple that danced across Leo's face. Pickett moved his hand in a feeble gesture, fumbling for the right words, but with a squeeze of his hand on his shoulder, Leo silenced him.

www.ingramcontent.com/pod-product-compliance
Lightning Source LLC
Chambersburg PA
CBHW020654260626
47157CB00008B/3028